BEFORE H|

(A MACKENZIE WHITE

BLAKE PIERCE

ISBN: 978-1-63291-870-3

BOOKS BY BLAKE PIERCE

PROLOGUE

Pam took a seat on the fallen log at the edge of the campsite and lit up a cigarette, energized after sex. Behind her, Hunter's tent was set up in a dented dome shape. She could hear him snoring lightly inside. Even here in the woods, it was the same; here she was, awake and energized in the afterglow of their lovemaking, while he was dead asleep. Here in the woods, though, she didn't mind so much.

She dug a little hole in the ground for the ashes of her cigarette, well aware that smoking in the forest during what had so far been a dry autumn was pretty reckless. She stared up into the sky, looking at the stars. It was a very cool night, as fall had staked its claim on the East Coast and dropped the temperatures significantly, and she hugged her shoulders against it. She wished Hunter's tent had one of those netted tops where you could look out, but no such luck. Still, there had been something romantic about it—getting away from home, being alone in the forest. It was the closest to living together she'd allow until the idiot finally proposed. Given the night sky, the perfect weather, and their crazy chemistry, it was one of the happier nights she'd had.

She wanted to go back inside, to warm up against him, but first she needed to go to the bathroom. She edged into the woods and took a moment to get her bearings. It was hard to make out where she was headed now that it was dark; the starlight and half-full moon provided some light, but not enough. She studied the layout around her and was pretty sure she just needed to cut hard to the left to find the rest area.

She crept out a few feet further and went in that direction for about thirty seconds. When she turned around she could not see the tent.

"Damn," she breathed, now starting to panic.

Get a grip, she told herself as she continued to walk. *The tent is right back there and—*

Her left foot caught on something, and before she was aware of what had happened, she was falling to the ground. She managed to throw her hands out at the last second, keeping her face from striking the ground. The wind went out of her in a solid little gasp and she pushed herself up right away, embarrassed.

She looked back to the log she had tripped over, angry at it in an almost childlike way. In the dark, the shape looked odd and

4

almost abstract. She knew one thing for certain, though. It was not a log.

It had to be the night playing tricks on her eyes. It *had* to be some weird play of the shadows in the dark.

But as a cold fear crept over her, she knew it for what it was. There was no denying it.

A human leg.

And from what she could tell, that's *all* it was. There did not appear to be a body to go along with it. It lay there on the ground, partially hidden by foliage and other woodland debris. The foot was covered in a running shoe and a sock that was soaked in blood.

Pam let out a scream. And as she turned and ran back through the black of night, she never stopped screaming.

CHAPTER ONE

Mackenzie sat in the passenger seat of a bureau-issued sedan with a standard-issue Glock in her hand—a weapon that was becoming as familiar to her as the feeling of her own skin. But today, it felt different. After today, *everything* would be different.

It took the voice of Bryers to break her from her mini-trance. He was sitting in the driver's seat, looking at her in a way that Mackenzie thought was similar to the stare of a disappointed father.

"You know…you don't have to do this," Bryers said. "No one is going to think any less of you if you sit this out."

"I think I *do* have to. I think I owe it to myself."

Bryers sighed and looked out of the windshield. In front of them, a large parking lot was illuminated in the night by weak streetlights that were positioned along the edges and in the center of the lot. There were three cars out there and Mackenzie could also see the shapes of three men, pacing anxiously.

Mackenzie reached out and opened the passenger side door.

"I'll be okay," she said.

"I know," Bryers said. "Just…please be careful. If anything happens to you tonight and the wrong people find out I was here with you—"

She didn't wait. She stepped out of the car and closed the door behind her. She held the Glock down low, walking casually into the parking lot toward the three men standing by the cars. She knew there was no reason to be nervous, but she was all the same. Even when she saw Harry Dougan's face among them, her nerves were still on edge.

"Did you *have* to have Bryers bring you?" one of the men asked.

"He's looking out for me," she said. "He doesn't particularly like any of you."

All three of the men laughed and then looked to the car Mackenzie had just gotten out of. They all waved to Bryers in perfect sync. In response, Bryers gave a fake smile and showed them his middle finger.

"He still doesn't even like me, huh?" Harry asked.

"Sorry. Nope."

The other two men looked to Harry and Mackenzie with the same resignation they had gotten used to over the last few weeks. While they weren't a *couple* per se, they were now close enough to cause the slightest bit of tension among their peers. The shorter of the men was a guy named Shawn Roberts and the other, a massive man who stood at six-foot-seven, was Trent Cousins.

Cousins nodded to the Glock in Mackenzie's hand and then unholstered his own from his hip.

"So are we going to do this?"

"Yeah, we probably don't have much time," Harry said.

They all looked around the parking lot in a conspiratorial fashion. An air of excitement started to thicken the air among them and as it did, Mackenzie came to a sudden realization: she was actually having fun. For the first time since her early childhood, she was legitimately excited for something.

"On three," Shawn Roberts said.

They all started swaying and bouncing on their feet as Harry started the countdown.

"One…two…three!"

In a flash, all four of them were off. Mackenzie took off to the left, headed for one of the three cars. Behind her, she already heard the gentle sound of shots being fired from the guns the others carried. These guns, of course, were mock-ups…paintball guns created to look and feel as close to the real thing as possible. This was not the first time Mackenzie had operated in a simulated munitions environment, but it *was* the first time she'd gone through one without an instructor—or pads of any kind.

To her right, a red smear of paint exploded on the pavement no more than six inches from her foot. She ducked behind the car and quickly slid to the front end of it. She dropped to her hands and knees and saw two different sets of feet separating further ahead of her, one of which was going behind another car.

Mackenzie had been scoping out the lay of the land while they were standing together. She knew that the best spot to be in the parking lot was going to be at the base of the stone pillar that held the streetlight in the center of the lot. Like the rest of Hogan's Alley, this parking lot was set up as randomly as possible, but with an eye toward educating academy trainees. Given that, Mackenzie knew there was always an optimal location for success in every setting. For this lot, it was that streetlight column. She'd not been able to get to it right away because there had already been two of the guys standing in front of it when Harry had counted down to three. But now she had to figure out how to make a run for it without getting hit.

She'd lose the game if she was shot. And there was five hundred dollars at stake here. She wondered how long ago this little pre-graduation ritual was implemented by trainees and how it had come to be a little hidden legend among the top of every class.

As these thoughts went through her head, she noticed that Harry and Cousins had engaged in a little back-and-forth shootout on the other side of the parking lot. Cousins was behind one of the cars and Harry was pressed against the side of a dumpster.

With a grin, Mackenzie took aim at Cousins. He was well hidden and she could not actually shoot him from where she was, but she could spook him. She aimed at the top corner of the car and fired. A blue spray of paint burst up as her shot landed dead on. She saw Cousins jerk back a bit, distracted from Harry. Harry, meanwhile, took advantage and fired off two shots.

She hoped he was keeping count. The whole point of their little unauthorized late-night exercise was to come out the only one not shot. Each player had the same weapon—a gun that fired paint pellets—and they were each only allowed the standard number of rounds that came with the sort of Glock their paint guns were modeled after. That meant they each had only fifteen rounds. Mackenzie now had fourteen left and she was pretty sure the three men had fired at least three or four each.

With Harry and Cousins occupied, that left only Shawn to contend with. But she had no idea where he was. To be so damn tall, he did a fine job of being stealthy.

She carefully got to her knees and lifted her head out from the side of the car, looking for Shawn. She did not see him, but she heard the little puff-like sound of a gun being fired nearby. She jerked back at the same moment a paint pellet struck the edge of the car's bumper. Some of the green paint splattered on her hand as she backed away but that did not count as a shot.

To be eliminated, you had to be shot in the arm, leg, back, or torso. The only thing that was off limits was headshots. Even though the pellets were small and made of thin plastic, they had been known to cause concussions. And if one took you in the eye, you could be blinded for life. That was one of the big reasons this little exercise was so frowned upon by the bureau. They knew it happened every year but they typically let the graduates have their little secret fun, turning a blind eye.

The shot gave Mackenzie a good idea of where Shawn was hiding, though. He was hunkered down behind the concrete post. And, just as she had planned for herself, he now had a great shot at just about anyone. He turned away from Mackenzie and fired off a quick shot at Harry. The shot missed, striking the top of the dumpster a few inches above Harry's head. He dropped to the ground as both Cousins and Shawn started firing at him.

Mackenzie attempted to get a shot off on Shawn and nearly took him in the shoulder. He ducked back down just as she fired, though, and the shot went wild. Meanwhile, she heard Cousins yell out in frustration and pain.

"I'm out," Cousins said, walking slowly to the edge of the lot. He sat down on a bench, where those who were eliminated were to sit in silence. Mackenzie saw a splotch of yellow paint on his ankle where Harry had landed a shot.

Harry took advantage of this distraction and dashed out from his hiding spot behind the dumpster. He was heading for the third parked car with his usual speed.

As he ran, Shawn rolled out from his hiding spot. He first fired at Mackenzie to keep her in hiding and then swiveled around to catch Harry. He fired another shot at Harry and it struck the ground about two inches away from Harry's left foot just as he leaped behind the car.

Mackenzie took the moment to move to the rear of the car, thinking she could draw Shawn out. She fired to the left of the concrete pillar, the same place she had aimed at while at the front end of the car. When the paint pellet exploded there, he waited a moment and then swiveled out with his eyes at the front of the car. When he did this, Mackenzie dashed out from the rear of the car and advanced quickly and quietly. When her angle was right, she fired off a shot that took him directly in the hip. Green paint exploded on his pants and shirt. He was so shocked by the attack that he fell back on his rear end.

"I'm out," Shawn yelled, giving Mackenzie a sour look.

No sooner had he started walking to the edge of the lot to join Cousins than Mackenzie saw a flicker of motion from her left.

Sneaky bastard, she thought.

She dropped to the ground and hunkered down behind the concrete post. The light shone bright above her head, like a spotlight. But she knew that this could work to her advantage when her attacker was in shadows. The light could be *too* bright, throwing off his aim the slightest little bit.

Just as she pressed her back against the concrete, she heard a paint pellet strike the back of the post. In the silence that followed, she heard Cousins and Shawn chuckling on the bench.

"This should be fun to watch," Cousins said.

"You say *fun,*" Shawn said. "I say painful."

Through their thin laughs, Mackenzie couldn't help but smile at the situation. She knew Harry would shoot her; they didn't have the type of relationship where he fawned all over her and would just let her win. They were both in the same boat—graduating tomorrow as new agents.

However, they had spent a lot of time together both in an academic setting and in friendlier situations. Mackenzie knew him well and knew what she needed to do to get him. Almost feeling bad for doing so, Mackenzie leaned out slowly and fired, striking the wheel on the car he was hiding behind.

He came out of hiding right away, popping up over the hood. She faked to the right, as if she were going back behind the post. Predictably, that's where he fired. Mackenzie reversed her direction and rolled to the left. She leveled out on her stomach, brought her gun up, and fired.

The shot took Harry in the right side of his chest. The yellow paint was almost as bright as the sun in the shadows he was hiding in.

Harry dropped his shoulders and tossed his gun out into the lot. He came out from around the car and shook his head, amazed.

"I'm out."

Mackenzie got to her feet and tilted her head, frowning at him.

"You mad?" she asked teasingly.

"Not at all. That was a sweet move."

Behind them, Cousins and Shawn were clapping. Further behind them, Bryers stepped out of his car and joined in. Mackenzie knew he had been worried about her but he'd also been honored to come with her. One part of the tradition to this exercise was that one seasoned agent had to tag along just in case something went wrong. It happened from time to time. The way Mackenzie had heard it, some guy had been hit in the back of the knee back in '99. He'd had to graduate on crutches.

Bryers joined them as they gathered together at the bench. He then reached into his pocket and withdrew the five hundred dollars that he had been holding for them—cash they had all contributed to the pot. He handed it over to Mackenzie and said:

"Was there really ever any doubt, guys?"

"Good work, Mac," Cousins said. "I'd rather it was you take me out than one of these jokers."

"Thanks, I think," Mackenzie said.

"I hate to sound like an old fart," Bryers said, "but it's nearly one in the morning. Get home and get some rest. All of you. Please don't come to graduation all tired and out of it."

That bizarre feeling of happiness spread through Mackenzie again. This was her group of friends—a group of friends she had come to know well ever since returning to a somewhat normal life following McGrath's little experiment with her nine weeks ago.

Tomorrow, they'd all be graduating from the academy, and, if everything shook out the way it was supposed to, they'd all be agents within the following week. While Harry, Cousins, and Shawn had no delusions about starting their careers off on illustrious cases, Mackenzie had more to look forward to…namely, the special group of agents McGrath had mentioned to her in the days following her last unexpected case. She still had no idea what that entailed, but she was excited about it nonetheless.

As their small group broke up and went on their separate ways, Mackenzie felt something else that she had not felt in quite some time. It was the sense that the future was still very much ahead of her, still unfolding and within her reach. And for the first time in a very long time, she felt like she had a great deal of control over the direction in which it was headed.

*

Mackenzie looked at the bruise on Harry's chest and even though she knew her first emotion should have been compassion, she couldn't help but laugh. The place where she had hit him was flaming red, the irritation spreading about two inches in all directions. It looked very much like a bee sting and, she knew, hurt much worse.

They were standing in her kitchen and she was wrapping an ice pack in a dishcloth for him. She handed it to him and he held it there comically. It was clear that he was embarrassed but also touched that she had invited him back to make sure he was okay.

"I'm sorry," she said sincerely. "But you know, maybe I can take you out for coffee on the winnings."

"That must be some damn good coffee," Harry said. He drew the ice pack away from his chest and scrunched up his nose when he looked down to the spot.

As Mackenzie watched him, she realized that although he had been to her apartment more than a dozen times and they had kissed on a few occasions, this was the first time he'd ever had his shirt off in her apartment. It was also the first time since Zack that she had seen a man this close to her partially undressed. Maybe it was the adrenaline from winning the contest or because of graduation tomorrow, but she liked it.

11

She stepped forward and placed her hand on the unharmed side of his chest, over his heart. "Does it still hurt?" she asked, stepping even closer.

"Not right now," he said, grinning nervously.

She slowly slid her hand over to the mark and touched it gingerly. Then, working only on the female instincts she had long ago shoved down and replaced with obligation and boredom, she leaned in and kissed it. She felt him tense up immediately. Her hand then found his side, pulling him closer to her. She kissed his collarbone, then the base of his shoulder, then his neck. He sighed and drew her even closer.

As was usually the case with them, they were kissing one another before either of them knew what was happening. It had only happened four previous times but each time, it had occurred like some force of nature, something unplanned and without any expectations.

It took less than ten seconds before he had her pressed lightly against the kitchen counter. Her hands explored his chest while his left hand found its way up her shirt. Her heart hammered in her chest and every muscle in her body told her that she wanted him, that she was ready for this.

They'd come close before—twice before, actually. But on both occasions, they had cut it off. Actually, *she* had stopped it. The first time, she had put an end to it just as he had started fumbling with the button on her pants. The second time, he'd been pretty drunk and she'd been far too sober. Neither of them had ever stated as such, but the hesitancy to sleep together came down to a mutual respect for one another and an uncertainty for the future. Also, she thought far too much of Harry to simply use him as a sexual release. She was growing more and more attracted to him, but sex had always been a very private matter. Before Zack, there had only been two men, and one of those had essentially been an issue of assault rather than mutual sex.

As all of this rocketed through her head while kissing Harry, she realized that her hands were now much lower than his chest. He apparently noticed this, too; he tensed up again and drew in a sharp breath.

She pulled her hands away suddenly and broke the kiss. She looked down to the floor, afraid that she'd see disappointment in his eyes.

"Wait," she said. "Harry…I'm sorry…I can't—"

"I know," he said, clearly a little frustrated and out of sorts. "I know it's—"

Mackenzie took one large collective breath and then stepped away from him. She turned away, unable to handle the confusion and hurt in his eyes. "We can't. I can't. I'm sorry."

"It's okay," he said, still clearly flustered. "Tomorrow is a big day and it's late. So I'm going to go before I have time to care that I've been shot down yet again."

She turned back around to face him and nodded. She didn't mind the barbed comments. She sort of deserved them.

"That might be for the best," she said.

Harry slid his shirt back on, complete with splattered paint, and slowly headed for the door. "Good job tonight," he said as he left. "There wasn't any doubt you'd come out the winner."

"Thanks," Mackenzie said, without much expression. "And Harry…really, I'm sorry. I don't know what's stopping me."

He shrugged as he opened the door. "It's okay," he said. "Just…I can't really do this much longer."

"I know," she said sadly.

"Goodnight, Mac."

He closed the door and Mackenzie was left alone. She stood in the kitchen, looking at the clock. It was 1:15 and she wasn't remotely tired. Maybe the little exercise at Hogan's Alley had driven too much adrenaline into her bloodstream.

Still, she tried going to bed but spent most of the night tossing and turning. In some sort of half-sleep state, she had dreams she barely remembered, but the one consistent thing to each of them was the face of her father, smiling, proud of her that she had made it this far—that she was graduating from the academy tomorrow.

But despite that smile, there was another consistent thing to the dreams, something she had long ago gotten used to as a frequent haunt once the lights went out and sleep came: the dead stare in his eyes and all of the blood.

CHAPTER TWO

Even though Mackenzie had set her alarm for eight o'clock, she was stirred awake by the vibrating of her cell phone at 6:45. She groaned as she came awake. *If this is Harry, apologizing for something he didn't even do, I'm going to kill him,* she thought. Still half-asleep, she grabbed her phone and read the display through hazy eyes.

She was relieved to see that it wasn't Harry, but Colby.

Puzzled, she answered it. Colby was not traditionally an early riser and they hadn't spoken in over a week. Anal retentive to the core, Colby was probably just freaking out about graduation and the uncertainty of the future. Colby was the one female friend Mackenzie had here in Quantico, so she had done whatever she could to make sure the friendship stuck—even if it meant answering an early call on the morning of graduation, after she'd only gotten four and a half broken hours of sleep the night before.

"Hey, Colby," she said. "What is it?"

"Were you asleep?" Colby asked.

"Yeah."

"Oh my God. I'm sorry. I figured you'd be up at the crack of dawn this morning, with everything that's going on."

"It's just graduation," Mackenzie said.

"Ha! I wish that's all it was," Colby said in a slightly hysterical voice.

"Are you all right?" Mackenzie asked, slowly sitting up in bed.

"I will be," Colby said. "Look…do you think you could meet me at the Starbucks on Fifth Street?"

"When?"

"As soon as you can get there. I'm heading out now."

Mackenzie did *not* want to go—she really didn't even want to get out of bed. But she had never heard Colby quite like this. And on such an important day, she figured she should try to be there for her friend.

"Give me about twenty minutes," Mackenzie said.

With a sigh, Mackenzie got out of bed and took care of only the basics in terms of getting ready. She brushed her teeth, tossed on a hooded sweatshirt and running pants, put her hair in a sloppy ponytail, and then headed out.

As she walked the six blocks down to 5th Street, the weight of the day started to sit on her. She was graduating from the FBI academy today, just before noon, nestled in the top five percent of her class. Unlike most of the graduates she had gotten to know over the last twenty weeks or so, she would not have any family in attendance to help her celebrate this accomplishment. She would be on her own, as she had been for most her life, since the age of sixteen. She was trying very hard to convince herself that it didn't bother her, but it did. It did not create sadness within her, but a weird sort of angst that was so old its edges had become dulled.

As she reached the Starbucks, she even noticed that traffic was a little thicker than usual—probably the family and friends of other graduates. She let it slide right off her back, though. She had spent the last ten years of her life trying not to give a damn about what her mother and sister thought of her, so why start now?

When she stepped into the Starbucks, she saw that Colby was already there. She was sipping from a cup and staring contemplatively out the window. There was another cup in front of her; Mackenzie assumed it was for her. She took a seat across from Colby and made a show of how tired she was, narrowing her eyes in a grumpy fashion as she took the seat.

"This is mine?" Mackenzie asked, taking the second cup.

"Yes," Colby said. She looked tired, sad, and all around grumpy.

"So what's wrong?" Mackenzie asked, skipping any attempt Colby might have of beating around the bush.

"I'm not graduating," Colby said.

"What?" Mackenzie asked, genuinely surprised. "I thought you passed everything with flying colors."

"I did. It's just...I don't know. Just being in the academy burned me out."

"Colby...you can't be serious."

Her tone had come with some force but she didn't care. This was not like Colby at all. Such a decision had come with some soul-searching. This was not a fluke, not some drama-filled last gasp of a woman plagued with nerves.

How could she just quit?

"But I am serious," Colby said. "I haven't really been passionate about it for the last three weeks or so. I'd go home some days and cry by myself because I felt trapped. I just don't want it anymore."

Mackenzie was stunned; she hardly knew what to say.

"Well, the day of graduation is one hell of a time to make this decision."

Colby shrugged and looked back out the window. She looked beaten. Defeated.

"Colby...you can't drop out. Don't do that." What was on the tip of her tongue but she did not say was: *If you quit now, these last twenty weeks mean nothing. It also makes you a quitter.*

"Ah, but I'm not really dropping out," Colby said. "I'll go to graduation today. I have to, actually. My parents came up from Florida so I sort of have to. But after today, that'll be it."

When Mackenzie had started the academy, the instructors had warned them that the drop-out rate among potential agents during the twenty-week academy session was around twenty percent—and had been as high as thirty in the past. But to think of Colby among those numbers simply didn't make sense.

Colby was too strong—too determined. How the hell could she be making such a decision so easily?

"What will you do?" Mackenzie asked. "If you actually leave all of this behind, what do you plan to do for a career?"

"I don't know," she said. "Maybe something along the lines of preventing human trafficking. Research and resources or something. I mean, I don't *have* to be an agent, right? There's plenty of other options. I just don't want to be an agent."

"You're actually serious about this," Mackenzie said dryly.

"I am. I just wanted to let you know now because after graduation, my parents will be fawning all over me."

Oh, you poor thing, Mackenzie thought, sarcastically. *That must be so terrible.*

"I don't get it," Mackenzie said.

"I don't expect you to. You're awesome at this. You love it. I think you were built for it, you know? Me...I don't know. Crash and burn, I guess."

"God, Colby...I'm sorry."

"No need to be," she said. "Once I send Mom and Dad back to Florida, all the pressure will be off. I'll tell 'em I just wasn't cut out for whatever bullshit assignment I was handed off the bat. And then it's off to whatever I want, I guess."

"Well...good luck, I guess," Mackenzie said.

"None of that, please," Colby said. "You're graduating in the top five percent today. Don't you dare let my drama bring you down. You've been a very good friend, Mac. I wanted you to hear this from me now rather than just noticing that I wasn't around in a few weeks."

Mackenzie made no attempt to hide her disappointment. She hated to feel like she was resorting to childish tactics, but she remained silent for a while, sipping on her coffee.

"How about you?" Colby asked. "Any family or friends coming up?"

"None," Mackenzie said.

"Oh," Colby said, a little embarrassed. "I'm sorry. I didn't know—"

"No need to apologize," Mackenzie said. It was now her turn to look blankly out the window when she added: "I sort of like it this way."

***

Mackenzie was underwhelmed by graduation. It was really nothing more than a formalized version of her high school graduation and not quite as classy and formal as her college graduation. As she waited for her name to be called, she had plenty of time to reflect back on those graduations and how her family had seemed to fade further and further into the background with each one.

She could recall nearly crying while walking to the stage at her high school graduation, saddened by the fact that her father would never see her grow up. She'd known it through her teen years but it was a fact that struck her like a rock between the eyes as she had walked up to the stage to receive her diploma. It was not something that had stirred her as much in college. When she had walked the stage during her college graduation, she had done so with no family in the crowd. It was, she realized during the academy ceremony, the pivotal moment in her life when she decided once and for all that she preferred to be alone in most things in life. If her family had no interest in her, then she had no interest in them.

The ceremony ended without much fanfare and when it was over, she spotted Colby taking pictures with her mother and father on the other side of the large lobby that the graduates and their guests all filed out into afterward. From what Mackenzie could tell, Colby was doing an excellent job of hiding her displeasure from her parents. All the while, her parents beamed proudly.

Feeling awkward and with nothing to do, Mackenzie started to wonder just how quickly she could get out of the assembly, get home and out of her graduation garb, and open the first of what would likely be several beers for the afternoon. As she started heading for the doors, she heard a familiar voice from behind her, calling her name.

"Hey, Mackenzie," the male voice said. She knew who it was at once—not just because of the voice itself, but because there were few people who called her *Mackenzie* in this environment rather than just *White.*

It was Ellington. He was dressed in a suit and looked just about as uncomfortable as Mackenzie felt. Still, the smile he gave her was a little *too* comfortable. Yet in that moment, she didn't really mind.

"Hi, Agent Ellington."

"I think in a situation like this, it's okay to call me Jared."

"I prefer Ellington," she said with a brief smile of her own.

"How do you feel?" he asked.

She shrugged, realizing just how badly she wanted to get out of there. She could tell herself all the lies she wanted, but the fact that she had no family, friends, or loved ones in attendance was starting to weigh on her.

"Just a shrug?" Ellington asked.

"Well, how *should* I feel?"

"Accomplished. Proud. Excited. Just to name a few."

"I'm all of those things," she said. "It's just...I don't know. The whole ceremony aspect of it seems a little much."

"I can understand that," Ellington said. "God, I hate wearing a suit."

Mackenzie was about to come back with a comment—maybe about how he actually wore the suit well—when she saw McGrath approaching from behind Ellington. He also smiled at her but, unlike Ellington's, his seemed nearly forced. He extended his hand to her and she took it, surprised at how limp his grip was.

"I'm glad you made it through," McGrath said. "I know you have a bright and promising career ahead of you."

"No pressure or anything, right?" Ellington said.

"The top five percent," McGrath said, not allowing Mackenzie a chance to say a single word. "Damn fine work, White."

"Thank you, sir," was all she could find to say.

McGrath leaned in close, all business now. "I'd like for you to come to my office Monday morning at eight o'clock. I wanted to get you deep inside the inner workings as soon as possible. I already have your paperwork drafted up—I actually took care of that a long time ago, so it would all be ready when this day came. That's how much faith I have in you. So...let's not wait. Monday at eight. Sound good?"

"Of course," she said, surprised at this uncharacteristic display of glowing support.

He smiled, shook her hand again, and quickly disappeared into the crowd.

When McGrath was gone, Ellington gave her a perplexed look and a wide grin.

"So, he's in good spirits. And I can tell you that doesn't happen very often."

"Well, it's a big day for him, I guess," Mackenzie said. "A whole new talent pool for him to pick and choose from."

"That's true," Ellington said. "But all jokes aside, the man is really smart with how he utilizes new agents. Keep that in mind when you meet with him on Monday."

An awkward silence passed between them; it was a silence that they had gotten used to and that had become a staple of their friendship—or whatever it was that was going on between them.

"Well, look," Ellington said. "I just wanted to say congrats. And I wanted to let you know that you're always welcome to call me if things get too real. I know that sounds dumb but at some point—even for the infamous Mackenzie White—you're going to need someone to vent to. It can catch up to you pretty quickly."

"Thanks," she said.

Then, suddenly, she wanted to ask him to come with her—not in any sort of romantic way, but just to have a familiar face with her. She knew him relatively well and even though she had conflicted feelings about him, she wanted him by her side. She hated to admit it, but she was starting to feel that she should do *something* to celebrate this day and this moment in her life. Even if it was just spending a few awkward hours with Ellington, it would be better (and likely more productive) than sitting around feeling sorry for herself and drinking alone.

But she said nothing. And even if she could have mustered the courage, it would not have mattered; Ellington quickly gave her a little nod and then, like McGrath, slipped back into the crowd.

Mackenzie stood there for a moment, doing her best to shrug off the increasing feeling of being utterly alone.

CHAPTER THREE

When Mackenzie showed up to her first day of work on Monday, she could not shake Ellington's words, running through her head like a mantra: *The man is really smart with how he utilizes new agents. Keep that in mind when you meet with him on Monday.*

She tried to use that to ground herself because if she was being truthful, she was nervous. It didn't help that her morning began when she was met by one of McGrath's men, Walter Hasbrook, now her department supervisor, and he escorted her like a child to the elevators. Walter looked to be pushing sixty and was roughly thirty pounds overweight. He had no personality and while Mackenzie held nothing against him, she didn't like the way he explained everything to her as if she were stupid.

This did not change as he led her to the third floor, where a maze of cubicles spread out like a zoo. Agents were posted at each cubicle, some talking on the phone while others typed into their computers.

"And this is you," Hasbrook said, gesturing to a cubicle in the center of one of the outer rows. "This is the central for Research and Surveillance. You'll find a few e-mails waiting for you, giving you access to the servers and a bureau-wide contact list."

She stepped into her cubicle, feeling a little disenchanted but still nervous. No, this was not the exciting case she'd hoped to start her career on but it was still the first step on a journey toward everything she'd been working for ever since she'd gotten out of high school. She pulled her rolling chair out and plopped down in her seat.

The laptop sitting in front of her was hers now. It was one of the bullet items Hasbrook had gone over with her. The desk was hers, the cubicle, the whole space. It wasn't exactly glamorous, but it was *her* space.

"In your e-mail, you'll find the details of your first assignment," Hasbrook said. "If I were you, I'd start on it right away. You'll want to call the case's supervising agent to coordinate, but you should be deep into it by the end of the day."

"Got it," she said, turning on the computer. Part of her was still angry with being saddled with a desk job. She'd wanted something in the field. After all McGrath had told her, that's what she'd been expecting.

No matter how great of a history you have, she told herself, *you can't expect to start out an all-star. Maybe this is your way of having to pay your dues—or McGrath's way of showing you who's boss and putting you in your place.*

Before Mackenzie could respond any more to his dry and monotone instructions, Hasbrook had already turned away. He was headed back to the elevators quickly, as if he were happy to be done with the day's minuscule chore.

When he was gone and she was alone in her cubicle she logged in to her computer and wondered why she was so damned nervous.

It's because this is it, she thought. *I worked hard to get here and it's finally mine. All eyes are on me now so I can't mess up— even if it's some random desk job.*

She checked her e-mail and fired off the necessary responses to get started on her assignment. Within an hour, she had all of the necessary documents and resources. She was determined to do her best, to give McGrath every reason to see that he was wasting her talent by having her ride a desk.

She pored over maps, cell phone records, and GPS data, working to pinpoint the location of two potential suspects involved in a sex trafficking ring. Within an hour or so of getting deeply involved, she found herself committed to it. The fact that she was not out on the street actively working to bring men like this down did not bother her in that moment. She was focused and she had a goal in mind; that's all she needed.

Yes, it was menial and borderline boring, but she would not let that hinder her work. She broke for lunch and came back to it, working with fervor and getting results. When the day came to a close, she e-mailed the department supervisor her results and headed out. She had never had an office job before but that's very much what this felt like. The only thing missing was the time clock to punch her card.

By the time she got to her car, she allowed herself to wallow in the disappointment again. A desk job. Stuck behind a computer and trapped between cubicle walls. This was not what she had envisioned.

Despite this, she was proud to be where she was. She wouldn't let ego or high expectations derail the fact that she was now an FBI agent. She couldn't help but think of Colby, though. She wondered where Colby was right now and what she'd have to say if she discovered that Mackenzie had been assigned a desk job to start off her career.

And a small part of Mackenzie couldn't help but wonder if Colby, having made her own decision to leave, had been the smarter of the two.

21

Would she ride this desk for years?

***

Mackenzie showed up the next morning determined to have a good day. She'd made some great progress on her case the day before and felt that if she could provide prompt and efficient results, McGrath would take notice.

Right away, she found that she had been bounced to another case. This one involved green card fraud. The attachments to the e-mails provided her with more than three hundred pages of testimonies, government files and documents, and legal jargon to use as resources. It looked incredibly tedious.

Fuming, Mackenzie looked to the phone. She had access to the servers, which meant she could get McGrath's number. She wondered how he'd respond if she called him and asked why she was being punished in such a way.

She talked herself out of it, though. Instead, she printed off every single document and created different stacks and piles on her desk.

Twenty minutes into this mind-numbing task, she heard a small knock at the entrance to her cubicle. When she turned around and saw McGrath standing there, she froze for a moment.

McGrath smiled at her in the same way he had approached her following graduation. Something in that smile told her that he honestly had no idea that she might feel demeaned by being stuck in a cubicle.

"Sorry it's taken me so long to get to you," McGrath said. "But I just wanted to come by and see how you're getting along."

She bit back the first several responses that came to mind. She gave a half-hearted shrug and said: "I'm doing fine. Just…well, I'm just a little confused."

"How so?"

"Well, on a few separate occasions, you told me that you couldn't wait to have me as an active agent. I guess I just didn't think that would involve sitting behind a desk and printing green card documents."

"Ah, I know, I know. But trust me. There's a rhyme and a reason to it all. Just stick your head down and forge head. Your time will come, White."

In her head, she heard Ellington's voice again. *The man is really smart with how he utilizes new agents.*

If you say so, she thought.

"We'll touch base soon," McGrath said. "Until then, take care."

Like Hasbrook the day before, McGrath seemed to be in a huge hurry to get away from the cubicles. She watched him go, wondering what sort of lesson or skills she was supposed to be picking up. She hated to feel entitled, but God…

What Ellington had said about McGrath…was she really supposed to believe that? Thinking of Ellington, she wondered if he knew what sort of detail she was on. She then thought of Harry and felt guilty for not calling him over the last few days. Harry had stayed quiet because he knew that she hated to feel pressured. It was one of the reasons she continued to see him. No man had ever really been this patient with her. Even Zack had his breaking point and the only reason they had lasted as long as they had was because they had gotten comfortable with one another and didn't want to be bothered with the inconvenience of change.

Mackenzie made the final stack of papers just as noon came around. Before diving into the madness waiting for her in the forms and notes, she figured she'd go out to grab lunch and a very large coffee.

She made her way down the hall and to the elevators. When the elevator arrived and the doors slid open, she was surprised to find Bryers on the other side. He seemed surprised to see her but smiled widely.

"What are you up to?" she asked.

"I was actually coming to see you. I thought you might want to grab lunch."

"That's where I was headed. Sounds great."

They took the elevator down together and grabbed a table at a little delicatessen a block down the street. When they were sitting down with their sandwiches, Bryers asked a very loaded question.

"How's it going?" he asked.

"It's…well, it's going. Stuck behind a desk, trapped in a cubicle, and reading over endless reams of paper isn't exactly what I had in mind."

"Coming from any other brand new agent, that might come off as sounding spoiled," Bryers said. "But, as it just so happens, I agree. You're being wasted. That's why I'm here: I've come to rescue you."

She looked up at him, wondering.

"What sort of rescue?"

"Another case," Bryers answered. "I mean, now, if you want to stay on your current workload and keep studying up on immigration fraud, I understand. But I think I've got something that is more within your interests."

She felt her heart start to beat faster.

"You can just pull me off of this?" she asked, suspicious.

"Indeed I can. Unlike last time, you have everyone's full support. I got the call from McGrath half an hour ago. He's not a *huge* fan of you jumping right into the action, but I twisted his arm a bit."

"Really?" she asked, feeling relieved and, as Bryers had indicated, just a little spoiled.

"I can show you my call history if you want. He was going to call and tell you himself but I asked for the favor of being the one to tell you. I think he knew ever since yesterday that you'd end up on this but we wanted to make sure we had a solid case."

"And you do?" she asked. A small ball of excitement started to grow in the pit of her stomach.

"Yes, we do. We found a body in a park in Strasburg, Virginia. It very closely resembles a body we found around the same area close to two years ago."

"You think they're linked?"

He waved off her question and took a mouthful of sandwich.

"I'll tell you about it on the way. For now, let's just eat. Enjoy the silence while you can."

She nodded and nibbled at her sandwich, although she was suddenly not very hungry at all.

She felt excitement, but also dread, and sadness. Someone had been murdered.

And it was going to be up to her to make things right.

CHAPTER FOUR

They left Quantico immediately after lunch. As Bryers drove, headed southwest, Mackenzie felt like she was being rescued from boredom, only to be brought to certain danger.

"So what can you tell me about this case?" she finally asked.

"A body has been discovered in Strasburg, Virginia. The body was found in a state park, in a condition that resembled a body that was discovered very close to the same area about two years ago."

"You think they're linked?"

"Has to be, if you want my opinion. Same location, same brutal style of murder. The files are in my bag in the back seat if you want to have a look."

She reached into the back seat and grabbed the portfolio-style case Bryers usually carried with him when there was going to be research involved. She slid a single folder out of it, continuing to ask questions as she did.

"When was this second body discovered?" she asked.

"Sunday. So far we haven't a trace of anything to point us in any direction. This is *not* a trail, like last time. We need you."

"Why me?" she asked, curious.

He looked back, curious himself.

"You're an agent now—and a damned good one at that," he said. "People are already whispering about you, people that didn't quite know who you were when you first came to Quantico. While it's atypical for a new agent to land a case like this, well, you aren't exactly a typical agent, now are you?"

"Is that a good thing or a bad thing?" Mackenzie asked.

"That depends on how you perform, I guess," he said.

She let things rest there, turning her attention to the folder. Bryers snuck a few peeks as she made her way through the contents—either to gauge her reaction or to see what she was currently looking at. As she made her way through the folder, he narrated the case.

"It took only a few hours before we were pretty sure the murder was linked to another body that was discovered about thirty-five miles away nearly two years ago. The pictures you see in the folder are from that body."

"Two years ago," Mackenzie said suspiciously. In the picture, she saw a body that had been badly mutilated. It was so bad, she had to look away for a moment. "How would you so easily link the two murders with such a huge expanse of time between them?"

25

"Because both bodies were found in the same state park and in the same very butchered condition. And you know what we say about coincidences in the bureau, right?"

"That they don't exist?"

"Exactly."

"Strasburg," Mackenzie said. "I'm not familiar with it all. Small town, right?"

"Eh, close to medium-sized. Population of around six thousand. One of those southern towns that's still clinging hard to the Civil War."

"And there's a state park out there?"

"Oh yeah," Bryers said. "That was news to me, too. Pretty big one, too. Little Hill State Park. About seventy miles of land all told. It damn near creeps in to Kentucky. It's popular for fishing, camping, and hiking. A lot of unexplored forest. That kind of state park."

"How were the bodies discovered?" Mackenzie asked.

"A camper found the latest one on Saturday night," Bryers said. "The body that was discovered two years ago was a pretty gruesome scene. The body was discovered weeks after the murder. There were rotting factors and some of the wildlife had taken some nibbles, as you see in the pictures."

"Any clear indication of how they were murdered?"

"Not that we can identify. The bodies were mutilated pretty badly. The first one two years ago—the head had been mostly severed, all ten fingers were cut off and never found, and the right leg was missing from the knee down. This most recent one was sort of spread all over the place. The left leg was discovered two hundred feet away from the rest of the body. The right hand was severed and has yet to be found."

Mackenzie sighed, overwhelmed for a moment by the evil in the world.

"That's brutal," she said softly.

He nodded.

"It is."

"You're right," she said. "The similarities are too eerie to ignore."

He stopped here and let out a huge cough, which he covered with the inside of his elbow. It was a deep cough, one of the long and dry ones that often come directly following a nasty cold.

"You okay?" she asked.

"Yeah, I'm fine. Fall is on the way. My stupid allergies flare up every year at this time. But how about *you*? Are you okay?

26

Graduation is over, you're now officially an agent, and the world is your proverbial oyster. Does that excite or terrify you?"

"A bit of both," she said honestly.

"Any family come up to see you on Saturday?"

"No," she said. And before he even had time to make a sad face or to express his regrets, she added: "But that's fine. My family was never really very close."

"I hear that," he said. "Same thing here. My folks were good people but I became a teenager and started *acting* like a teenager and then they sort of shrugged me off. I wasn't Christian enough for them. Liked girls a little too much. That sort of thing."

Mackenzie said nothing because she was in a bit of shock. It was the most he had said about himself since she had known him—and it had all come in a sudden, unexpected, twelve-second burst.

Then, before she was aware that she was even doing it, she spoke up again. And when the words were out of her mouth, she almost felt like she had vomited.

"My mom sort of did that to me," she said. "I got older and she saw that she wasn't really in control of me anymore. And if she couldn't control me, then she didn't want much to do with me. But when she lost that control over me, she lost control over just about everything else, too."

"Ah, aren't parents grand?" Bryers said.

"In their own special way."

"How about your father?" Bryers asked.

The question was like a sting to the heart but she again surprised herself by answering. "He's dead," she said with a crisp tone to her voice. Still, a part of her wanted to tell him about her father's death and how she had discovered the body.

While their time apart had seemed to improve their working relationship, she still wasn't quite ready to share those wounds with Bryers. Still, despite her cold answer, Bryers now seemed much more open, talkative, and willing to engage. She wondered if it was because he was now working with her with the assurance and blessing of those that supervised him.

"Sorry to hear it," he said, passing over it in a way that let her know he'd picked up on her unwillingness to talk about it. "My folks…they didn't understand why I wanted this for a job. Of course, they were very strict Christians. When I told them that I did not believe in God when I was seventeen, they basically gave up on me. Since then, I've seen both of my parents to the grave. Dad hung in there for about six years after mom passed. Dad and I made some

27

unstable sort of peace after mom died. We were friendly again before he died of lung cancer in 2013."

"At least you got a chance to patch things up," Mackenzie said.

"True," he said.

"Did you ever get married? Any kids?"

"I was married for seven years. I got two daughters out of it. One is in college in Texas right now. The other is somewhere in California. She stopped talking to me ten years ago, right after she left high school, got knocked up and engaged to a twenty-six-year-old."

She nodded, finding the conversation too awkward to continue. It was odd that he was opening up to her in such a way, but she appreciated it. Some of what he had told her made some sense, though. Bryers was a fairly solitary man, and that lined up with having had a strained relationship with his parents.

The information about two daughters that he rarely spoke to, though—that had been a huge revelation. It made some sort of sense as to why he was so open with her and why he seemed to enjoy working with her.

The next two hours were filled with scant conversation, mostly about the case at hand and Mackenzie's time in the academy. It was nice to have someone to talk to about such things and it made her feel a little guilty for shutting him down he had asked about her father.

It was another hour and fifteen minutes before Mackenzie started seeing signs announcing the exit for Strasburg. Mackenzie could practically feel the air within the car shifting as they both switched gears, tucking personal matters away and focusing solely on the job at hand.

Six minutes later, Bryers turned the sedan onto the Strasburg exit. When they entered the town, Mackenzie felt herself tense up. But it was a good sort of tension—the same kind she had felt as she had stepped into the parking lot the night before graduation with the paintball gun in her hand.

She had arrived. Not just in Strasburg, but into a stage of her life she had dreamed about ever since taking her first demeaning desk job back in Nebraska before she'd been given a proper chance.

My God, she thought. *Was that only five and a half years ago?*

Yes, it was. And now that she was literally being driven toward the realization of all of those dreams, the five years that separated that desk job from the current moment in the passenger seat of Bryers's car seemed like a barricade of sorts that kept those two sides of her apart. And that was just as well as far as Mackenzie was concerned. Her past had never done anything but hold her back, and now that she had finally seemed to outrun it, she was glad to leave it dead and rotting in the past.

She saw the sign for Little Hill State Park, and as he slowed the car, her heart quickened. Here she was. Her first case while officially on the job. All eyes would be on her, she knew.

The time had come.

CHAPTER FIVE

When Mackenzie stepped out of the car in the Little Hill State Park visitor's lot, she braced herself, feeling immediately the tension of murder in the air. She did not understand how she could sense it, but she could. It was a sort of sixth sense she had that sometimes she wished she hadn't. No one else she had ever worked with seemed to have it, too.

In a way, she realized, they were lucky. It was a blessing, but also a curse.

They walked across the lot and to the visitor's center. While fall had not yet fully gripped Virginia yet, it was making its presence known early. The leaves all around them were beginning to turn, teasing an array of reds, yellows, and golds. A security shack sat behind the center, and a bored-looking woman regarded them from the shack with a wave.

The visitor's center was a lackluster tourist trap at best. A few clothing racks displayed T-shirts and water bottles. A small shelf along the right side contained maps of the area and a few brochures on fishing tips. In the center of it all was a single older woman a few years beyond retirement, smiling at them from behind a counter.

"You folks are with the FBI, right?" the woman asked.

"That's right," Mackenzie said.

The woman gave a quick nod and picked up the landline phone sitting behind the counter. She punched a number in from a scrap of paper sitting by the phone. As she waited, Mackenzie turned away and Bryers followed.

"You said you haven't spoken directly with the Strasburg PD, right?" she asked.

Bryers shook his head.

"Are we walking in as friends or an obstacle?"

"I guess we'll have to see."

Mackenzie nodded as they turned back to the counter. The woman had just hung up the phone and was looking to them again.

"Sheriff Clements will be here in about ten minutes. He'd like for you to meet him at the guard shack outside."

They walked back outside and headed for the guard shack. Again, Mackenzie found herself nearly hypnotized by the colors blooming on the trees. She walked slowly, taking it all in.

"Hey, White?" Bryers said. "Are you okay?"

"Yeah. Why do you ask?"

"You're trembling. A little pale. As a seasoned FBI agent, my hunch is that you're nervous—*very* nervous."

She clenched her hands together tightly, aware that there was indeed a slight tremor in her hands. Yes, she *was* nervous but she had hoped she was hiding it. Apparently, she was doing a very poor job.

"Look. You're into the real deal now. You can be nervous. But work *with* it. Don't fight it or hide it. I know that sounds counterintuitive but you have to trust me on this."

She nodded, a little embarrassed.

They continued on without saying another word, the wild colors of the trees around them seeming to press in. Mackenzie looked ahead to the guard shack, eyeing the bar that hung from the shack and across the road. As cheesy as it seemed, she could not help but feel her future was waiting for her on the other side of that bar and she found herself equally intimidated and anxious to cross it.

Within seconds, they both heard the small engine noise. Almost immediately after that, a golf cart came into view, coming around the bend. It looked to be going at top speed and the man behind the wheel was practically hunched over it, as if willing the cart to go faster.

The cart sped forward and Mackenzie got her first glimpse of the man she assumed to be Sheriff Clements. He was a forty-something hard-ass. He had the glassy stare of a man who had been dealt a rough hand in life. His black hair was just beginning to go gray at the temples and he had the sort of five o'clock shadow bordering his face that looked like it was probably always there.

Clements parked the cart, barely regarded the guard in the shack, and walked around the bar to meet Mackenzie and Bryers.

"Agents White and Bryers," Mackenzie said, offering her hand.

Clements took it and shook it passively. He did the same to Bryers before turning his attention back to the paved trail he had just come down.

"If I'm being honest," Clements said, "while I certainly appreciate the bureau's interest, I'm not so sure we need the assistance."

"Well, we're here now, so we may as well see if we can lend a hand," Bryers said, being as friendly as he could.

"Well then, hop on the cart and let's see," Clements said. Mackenzie was trying her best to size him up as they loaded up on the cart. Her main concern from the start was trying to determine if

Clements was simply under immense stress or if he was just as ass by nature.

She rode alongside Clements in the front of the cart while Bryers clung to the back. Clements did not say a single word. It fact, it seemed like he was making an effort to let them both know that he felt inconvenienced by having to usher them around.

After a minute or so, Clements swerved the cart to the right where the paved road forked off. Here, the pavement ended and became an even thinner trail that barely allowed for the width of the cart.

"So what instructions has the guard at the guard shack been given?" Mackenzie asked.

"No one comes through," Clements said. "Not even park rangers or cops unless I've given prior permission. We already have enough people farting around out here, making things harder than it has to be."

Mackenzie took the not-too-subtle jab and tucked it away. She wasn't about to get into an argument with Clements before she and Bryers had gotten a chance to check out the crime scene.

Roughly five minutes later, Clements hit the brakes. He stepped out even before the cart had come to a complete stop. "Come on," he said, like he was talking to a child. "This way."

Mackenzie and Bryers stepped down from the cart. All around them, the forest loomed high over them. It was beautiful but filled with a sort of thick silence that Mackenzie had come to recognize as an omen of sorts—a signal that there was bad blood and bad news in the air.

Clements led them into the woods, walking quickly ahead of them. There was no real trail to speak of. Here and there Mackenzie could see signs of old footpaths winding through the foliage and around the trees but that was it. Without realizing she was doing so, she took the lead in front of Bryers as she tried to keep up with Clements. On occasion, she had to swat away a low-hanging branch or wipe away stray strands of cobwebs from her face.

After walking for two or three minutes, she started to hear several mingled voices. The sounds of movement grew louder and she started to understand what Clements had been talking about; even without seeing the scene, Mackenzie could tell that it was going to be overcrowded.

She saw proof of this less than a minute later as the scene came into view. Crime scene tape and small border flags had been set up in a large triangular shape within the forest. Among the yellow tape and red flags, Mackenzie counted eight people, Clements included. She and Bryers would make ten.

"See what I mean?" Clements asked.

Bryers came up beside Mackenzie and sighed. "Well, this is a mess."

Before stepping forward, Mackenzie did her best to survey the scene. Of the eight men, four were local PD, easily identified by their uniforms. There were two others that were in uniforms but of a different kind—state PD, Mackenzie assumed. Beyond that, though, she took in the scene itself rather than let the bickering distract her.

The location seemed to be random. There were no points of interest, no items that might be seen as symbolic. It was just like any other section of these forests in every way Mackenzie could see. She guessed that they were about a mile or so off of the central trail. The trees were not particularly thick here, but there was a sense of isolation all around her.

With the scene thoroughly taken in, she looked to the bickering men. A few looked agitated and one or two looked angry. Two of them weren't wearing any sort of uniform or outfit to denote their profession.

"Who are the guys not in uniform?" Mackenzie asked.

"Not sure," Bryers said.

Clements turned to them with a scowl on his face. "Park rangers," he said. "Joe Andrews and Charlie Holt. Shit like this happens and they think they're the police."

One of the rangers looked up with venom in his eyes. Mackenzie was pretty sure Clements had nodded this man's way when he'd said *Joe Andrews.* "Watch yourself, Clements. This is a state park," Andrews said. "You've got about as much authority out here as a gnat."

"That might be," Clements said. "But you know as well as I do that all I have to do is make a single call to the precinct and get some wheels moving. I can have you out of here within an hour, so just do whatever it is you need to do and get your ass out of here."

"You self-righteous little fu—"

"Come on," a third man said. This was one of the state cops. The man was built like a mountain and wore sunglasses that made him look like the villain from a bad '80s action movie. "I have the authority to throw both of you out of here. So stop acting like children and do your jobs."

This man noticed Mackenzie and Bryers for the first time. He walked over to them and shook his head almost apologetically.

"Sorry you're having to hear all of this nonsense," he said as he approached. "I'm Roger Smith with the state police. Some scene we've got here, huh?"

"That's what we're here to figure out," Bryers said.

Smith turned back to the seven others and used a booming voice when he said: "Step back and let the feds do their thing."

"What about *our* thing?" the other ranger asked. *Charlie Holt,* Mackenzie remembered. He looked to Mackenzie and Bryers with suspicion. Mackenzie thought he even looked a little timid and afraid around them. When Mackenzie looked his way, he looked to the ground, bending over to pick up an acorn. He moved the acorn from hand to hand, then started to pick at the top of it.

"You've had enough time," Smith said. "Just back up for a second, would you?"

Everyone did as asked. The rangers in particular looked unhappy about it. Doing everything she could to ease the situation, Mackenzie figured it would help if she tried involving the rangers as much as possible so tempers didn't flare.

"What sort of information do rangers typically need to pull from something like this?" she asked the rangers as she ducked under the crime scene tape and started to look around. She saw a marker where the leg had been found, marked as such on a small clapboard marker. A good distance away she saw another marker where the remainder of the body had been found.

"We need to know how long to keep the park closed down for one thing," Andrews said. "As selfish as it might sound, this park accounts for a pretty good chunk of tourism revenue."

"You're right," Clements spoke up. "That *does* sound selfish."

"Well, I think we're allowed to be selfish from time to time," Charlie Holt said rather defensively. He then regarded Mackenzie and Bryers with a stare of contempt.

"Why's that?" Mackenzie asked.

"Do either of you happen to know what sort of crap we have to put up with out here?" Holt asked.

"No, actually," Bryers asked.

"Teenagers having sex," Holt said. "Full-blown orgies from time to time. Weird Wicca practices. I've even caught some drunk guy out here getting frisky with a stump—and I'm talking pants all the way down. These are the stories the Staties laugh about and the local PD just use as fodder for jokes on the weekends." He bent down and picked up another acorn, picking at it like he did with the first one.

"Oh," added Joe Andrews. "And then there's catching a father in the act of molesting his eight-year-old-daughter just off of a fishing path and having to stop it. And what thanks do I get? The girl yelling at me to leave her daddy alone and then a firm warning from local and state PD to not be so rough next time. So yeah…we can be selfish about our authority from time to time."

The forest went quiet then, broken only by one of the other local cops as they made a dismissive laughing sound and said: "Yeah. Authority. Right."

Both rangers stared the man down with extreme hatred. Andrews took a step forward, looking as if he might explode from rage. "Fuck you," he said simply.

"I said *stop this nonsense*," Officer Smith said. "One more time and every single one of you are out of here. You got it?"

Apparently, they did. The forest fell into silence again. Bryers stepped behind the tape with Mackenzie and when everyone else busied themselves behind them, he leaned over to her. She felt Charlie Holt's eyes on her and it made her want to punch him.

"This could get ugly," Bryers said quietly. "Let's do our best to get out of here post-haste, what do you say?"

She went to work then, combing the area and taking mental notes. Bryers had stepped out of the crime scene and was resting against a tree as he coughed into his arm. She did her best not to let this distract her, though. She kept her eyes to the ground, studying the foliage, the ground, and the trees. The one thing that made little sense to her was how a body in such bad shape had been discovered here. It was hard to tell how long ago the murder had occurred or the body had been dumped; the ground itself showed no signs of the brutal act being carried out.

She noted the location of the placards that marked where the different parts of the body had been found. It was too far apart to have been an accident. If someone dumped a mutilated body and placed the parts so far apart, that spoke on intentionality.

"Officer Smith, do you know if there were any signs of bite marks from possible wildlife on the body?" she asked.

"If there were, they were so minuscule that a basic exam didn't reveal any. Of course, when the autopsy comes in we'll know more."

"And no one on your crew or with local PD moved the body or the severed limbs?"

"Nope."

"Same here," Clements said. "Rangers, how about you guys?"

35

"No," said Holt with an evil sneer in his voice. He now seemed to be taking offense to just about everything.

"Can I ask why that might matter in terms of finding out who did it?" Smith asked her.

"Well, if the killer did his business here, there would be blood everywhere," Mackenzie explained. "Even if it happened a long while ago, there would be at least trace amounts scattered around. And I don't see any. So the other possibility is that he maybe dumped the body here. But if that's the case, why would a severed leg be so far away from the rest of the body?"

"I don't follow," Smith said. Behind him, she saw that Clements was also listening attentively but trying not to show it.

"It makes me think the killer *did* dump the body out here but he separated the parts so far apart on purpose."

"Why?" Clements asked, no longer able to pretend he wasn't listening.

"It could be several reasons," she said. "It could have been something as morbid as just having fun with the body, scattering it around like it was nothing but toys he was playing with. Wanting to get our attention. Or there could be some sort of calculated reasons for it—for the distance, for the fact that it was a leg, and so on."

"I see," Smith said. "Well, some of my men already wrote up a report that has the distance between the body and the leg. Just about every measurement you could ask for."

Mackenzie took a look around again—at the gathered group of men and the seemingly peaceful forest—and paused. There was no clear reason for this location. That made her think that the location was random. Still, to be so far off of the beaten path spoke of something else. It indicated that the killer knew these woods—maybe even the park itself—fairly well.

She started walking around the scene, looking closer for trace amounts of dried blood. But there was nothing. With every moment that passed, she became more and more certain of her theory.

"Rangers," she said. "Is there any way to get the names of people that frequent the park? I'm thinking about people that come here a lot and know the area well."

"Not really," Joe Andrews said. "The best we can do is provide a list of financial donors."

"That's not necessary," she said.

"You have a theory to test?" Smith asked.

"The actual murder was done elsewhere and the body was dumped here," she said, half to herself. "But why here? We're almost a mile away from the central path and there appears to be nothing significant about this location. So that makes me think that whoever is behind this knows the park grounds fairly well."

She got a few nods as she explained things but got the overall feeling that they either doubted her or just didn't really care.

Mackenzie turned to Bryers.

"You good here?" she asked.

He nodded.

"Thanks, gentlemen."

Everyone looked at her in silence. Clements seemed to be sizing her up.

"Well, come on then," Clements said, finally. "I'll give you a ride back to your car."

"No, that's okay," Mackenzie said a bit rudely. "I think I'd rather walk."

Mackenzie and Bryers took their exit, heading back through the woods and toward the walking trail Clements had brought them down.

As they sank back into the forest, the stares of the state police, Clements and his men, and the park rangers at their backs, Mackenzie couldn't help but appreciate the grand scale of the forest. It was eerie to think about how endless the possibilities were out here. She thought about what the ranger had said, about the countless crimes that took place in these forests, and something about that sent an icy chill through her.

If someone had it in them to slaughter people like the person who had been discovered within this taped-off triangle *and* they had a fairly decent knowledge of these forests, there were virtually no limits to the amount of menace they could cause.

And she felt sure that he would strike again.

CHAPTER SIX

Mackenzie settled down in her office just after six in the evening, exhausted from the long day and tidying up her notes to prepare for the debrief she had requested on their way back from Strasburg.

A knock came on her door and she looked up to find Bryers, looking as tired as she felt, holding a folder and a cup of coffee. He looked like he was trying his best to hide his exhaustion and it then occurred to her that he had been hands-off back in the state park, allowing her to take the lead with Clements, Smith, Holt, and the other egotistical men out in the forest. That, plus his coughing, made her wonder if he was coming down with something.

"The debrief is ready to roll," he said.

Mackenzie got up and followed him to the conference room at the end of the hall. When she entered, she glanced around at the several agents and experts that made up the team on the Little Hill State Park case. There were seven people in all and while she personally thought that was too much manpower for a case this early on, it was not her place to say such a thing. This was Bryers's and she was simply happy to be along for the ride. It was much better than reading up on immigration laws and swimming in paperwork.

"We have a busy day today," Bryers said. "So let's start things off with a quick recap."

If he *had* been tired when he came in, he had shrugged it off. Mackenzie watched and listened with rapt attention as Bryers filled in the seven people in the room with what he and Mackenzie had discovered in the woods of Little Hill State Park that day. The others in the room took notes, some scribbling on pads, others typing it into tablets or smartphones.

"One thing to add," one of the other agents said. "I got a ping about fifteen minutes ago. The case has officially hit the local news. They've already started calling this guy the Campground Killer."

A moment of silence filled the room, and inwardly, Mackenzie sighed. This would make life much harder for them all.

"Man, that was fast," Bryers said. "Damned media. How in the hell did they get their hands on it so fast?"

No one answered, but Mackenzie thought she knew. A small town like Strasburg was filled with people who loved to hear their town's name on the news—even if it was for bad news. She could think of a few park rangers or local police that might fit into that category.

"Anyway," Bryers went on, undeterred, "the last piece of information we got came from the state PD. They handed off details of the crime scene to forensics. We now know that the severed leg and the body to which it was formerly attached were exactly three and a half feet apart. We obviously have no idea if that is significant, but we'll be looking into it. Also—"

A knock at the door interrupted him. Another agent dashed into the room and handed a folder to Bryers. He whispered something quickly to Bryers and then made his exit.

"The coroner's report from the newest body," Bryers said, opening up the folder and looking inside. He scanned it quickly and then started to pass the three sheets around to the team. "As you'll see, there were no marks from hungry predators on the body, though there were slight bruises along the back and shoulders. It's believed the leg and right hand were severed with a rather dull knife or some other large blade. The bones looked to have been more broken than sawed through. This differs from the case from two years ago but, of course, that could just be because the killer doesn't take care of his tools or weapons."

Bryers gave them all a moment to look at the report. Mackenzie barely looked it over, perfectly fine with relying on Bryers's rundown. She had already grown to trust him and while she knew the value of files and reports, there was nothing better than a straight verbal report as far as she was concerned.

"We also now know the name of the deceased: Jon Torrence, twenty-two years of age. He went missing about four weeks ago and was last seen at a bar in Strasburg. Some of you will have the not-so-fortunate task of speaking to his family members today. We've also dug up some information on the victim from two years ago. Agent White, would you like to fill the team in on that victim?"

Mackenzie had read the details in a document sent over from Officer Smith and his state PD team on their drive between Strasburg and Quantico. She'd memorized the details within ten minutes and, as such, was able to recite them to the team with confidence.

"The first body was that of Marjorie Leinhart. Her head was almost completely severed from her body. The killer cut off all of her fingers and her right leg from the knee down. None of the severed parts were ever discovered. At the time of her death, she was twenty-seven years old. Her mother was the only surviving relative as Marjorie was an only child and her father died while stationed in Afghanistan in 2006. But Mrs. Leinhart committed suicide a week after her daughter's body was discovered. Vigorous searches revealed only one other relative—an estranged uncle living in London—that knows nothing about the family. There were no boyfriends and the few close friends that were questioned all checked out. So there is literally no one to question there."

"Thank you, Agent White. So there you have it. That's all we have for right now. So I'm going to want some of you on family detail, one or two of you to help with forensics, and someone else to do some digging about any violent crimes in or around Little Hill State Park over the last twenty-five years or so. Does anyone else have anything to add?"

"This could be ritualistic," one of the older agents offered. "Dismemberment in such a capacity is telltale of ritualistic murders. I'd be interested to see if there have been any reports of Satanism or cultlike gatherings in or around Strasburg."

"Good point," Bryers said, making a quick note on one of his papers.

Mackenzie raised her hand. A few of the agents within the room—all seasoned and well-decorated—rolled their eyes. *Of course you have something to add,* they all seemed to think.

"Yes, Agent White?" Bryers asked. He gave her a knowing little smile as the rest of the room looked her way.

"Looking through some old case files that the state PD sent over, I found a documented case of a child abduction right around the Little Hill area nineteen years ago. A boy named Will Albrecht. He was taken right from under his parents' noses. When the parents were questioned, they stated that their son loved to ride his bike around the trails in Little Hill State Park. The connection is tenuous at best but, I think, worth looking into."

"Absolutely," Bryers said. "Can you make sure everyone on the team gets that file?"

"I'm on it," she said, already pulling the e-mail up on her phone.

"And why would that be relevant?" another agent asked.

Never one to back down from a challenge, Mackenzie answered right away. "I'm working on the theory that whoever did this knew the area well. To randomly dump a body in such a non-selective place speaks of a knowledge of the forest. Throw in Marjorie Leinhart from two years ago and that only backs it up further."

"I still don't see how that stacks up with a kidnapping," yet another agent said.

"To take a kid while his parents were very close by and get away with it...you'd have to know the lay of the land. They never even came *close* to finding the abductor."

That apparently gave them enough to dangle on. She got a few appreciative nods but most everyone else in the room simply looked to their phones or the table in front of them.

"Anything else?" Bryers asked. As he waited for a response, he let out a hearty cough into his elbow.

"That's it then," Bryers said after three seconds of silence. "Let's get to work and land ourselves a killer."

The team started to murmur and mumble excitedly as they filed out. Mackenzie stayed behind, curious to see if Bryers needed anything else before they called it a day.

"You know," Bryers said. "I'm going to task someone with looking into that abduction you mentioned. If it turns out to be nothing, you're going to have an enemy or two."

"So, business as usual?"

"I guess so," he said with a grin. "But you know...maybe you and I handle that detail. We'll drive back up to Strasburg tomorrow and kill two birds with one stone. We'll also talk to the family of Jon Torrence. You up for another drive out into the country?"

CHAPTER SEVEN

They arrived in Strasburg shortly after nine o'clock the following morning and as they drove into the town, Mackenzie thought she could understand the charm of a place like this. To be rooted so deeply in history had, to her, seemed a little silly at first. But there was also something rustic and respectable about it as well. American flags hung nearly everywhere (along with Confederate flags here and there, a staple of small-town Virginia, she assumed) and a lot of the local businesses had been named after Civil War troops.

Mackenzie knew that it was a foolish trap to think that the most deranged killers came from these sorts of unsuspecting towns. Statistics showed that a crazed killer was just as likely to step out of New York or LA as they were a small backwoods town in Virginia. Still, there was something quiet and just a bit morose about a town like this—a town where everything seemed perfect while passing through, making it easy to forget that there were dark secrets possibly hiding behind every charming little front door.

They finally pulled into the Torrences' driveway, and Mackenzie felt a knot tightening in her stomach. Mackenzie had called ahead while they were on the way and spoke to Pamela Torrence, Jon's mother. She'd seemed pleased to speak with anyone that could help and Mackenzie saw evidence of this as the front door of the small house opened up and Pamela stepped out before Bryers had even parked the car.

They met her on the front porch and made quick introductions. It was clear that Pamela Torrence had not gotten much sleep over the last few days. Her eyes looked dazed as there were red splotchy marks under them. Still, she was trying to be as normal as she could as she welcomed Mackenzie and Bryers into her home.

As she led them into her small living room, Mackenzie saw more stereotypes of the small-town American family. There were pictures of children on the walls and on top of end tables. One picture Mackenzie saw showed what she assumed was a teenaged Jon Torrence, smiling bright in his high school football uniform.

"Thanks for coming out," Pamela said.

"Of course," Mackenzie replied. "When I spoke to you on the phone, you indicated that your husband was here. Is he still around?"

"No," she said. "It's been too much for Ray. When he learned that you were coming, he started crying. He got it together, grabbed his rifle, and went out to go hunting."

Mackenzie didn't think that was the best idea, but she said nothing. Who was she to question the ways in which the parents of a recently dead young man chose to grieve?

"So what can you tell us about Jon?" Mackenzie asked.

Pamela shrugged and tried on a smile that didn't look as if it belonged on her tired face. "He was a good kid. A quiet kid. He was working part time at Gino's Pizza and taking classes over at the community college. He was only in his second year. He started late. He was always scared to go to college. He finally talked himself into it after the girl that he had dated for three years finally moved away after graduating from Virginia Tech."

"What did he do for fun?" Bryers asked.

"He had started to get into running. He did these little events here and there—five K races for breast cancer, church fundraisers, things like that. He had his eye on one of those mountain madness marathons early next year. He was training for that."

"Did he run in Little Hill Park often?" Mackenzie asked.

"Oh, yes," Pamela said. "It was his favorite place. He loved running out there. He went at least twice a week."

"What can you tell us about the girl that broke up with him?" Mackenzie asked. "Was there still a friendship after the break-up?"

"I don't think so," Pamela said. "If there was, he wasn't telling me."

"Do you think it's something he might have gone to your husband about?" Bryers asked.

"Probably not," Pamela said. "Jon and Ray were never close. I think it's one of the reasons Ray's taking it so hard. Too much regret…"

"You said Jon was working part time and going to community college," Mackenzie said. "Was he still living here or did he have a place of his own?"

"He was living here," she said. "He was so ashamed. We never asked for rent, but he gave us what he could every month."

"Would you mind if we had a look around his room?"

"Help yourselves."

Pamela led them downstairs into a partially finished basement. The area that had been finished consisted of a bathroom and a fairly spacious bedroom. Mackenzie and Bryers stepped inside to what was clearly the bedroom of an older and recently dumped male. An iPod sat on the floor around a few magazines; the magazines all appeared to be related to weaponry for hunting. Dirty clothes were scattered here and there and the bed was a mess.

A TV sat on top of a small dresser. An Xbox and several games and movies sat beside it. She saw a few romantic comedy titles alongside games like *Halo* and *Call of Duty*. She also saw a few sketchpads. She flipped through them and saw some fairly innocent sketches of nudes, renderings of deer and rifles, and a few attempts at drawing a woman's face. Mackenzie wondered if it was the face of his ex-girlfriend.

"Was he a big hunter like your husband?" Mackenzie asked, nodding to the magazines.

"He used to be. It was the one thing they used to try to do together. But they just never clicked, you know? Ray and some of his hunting buddies always made fun of him for going to college, for being into art in high school, for being loyal to one girl. That sort of dumb macho crap. Earlier this year there was a pretty big fight between Jon and one of the other guys in the hunting group."

"What kind of fight?"

"Fists were thrown," Pamela said. "I think Ray felt like he had to make a choice between his friends and a son he had never really seen eye to eye with. He chose his friends. And that's killing him right now."

"Do you know the name of the guy Jon fought with?" Mackenzie asked.

Pamela rolled her eyes. "Curtis Palmer," she said through clenched teeth. "A grade-A asshole if there ever was one. He's done some time before. Beating on his wife and kid and making them split town. That kind of thing."

Mackenzie and Bryers shared a look that Pamela seemed to lock in on. "I could give you his address if you need it," she said.

"Yes, I think that might be helpful," Mackenzie said.

"I'll go upstairs and write it down for you. Take your time down here."

When Pamela was headed back up the stairs, Bryers flipped through the games and movies. "What do you think?" he asked.

"I think Jon Torrence had a rough life and was in the wrong place at the wrong time. I think we can run some records to see if there are any connections—maybe between the ex-girlfriend and the first victim—but I doubt anything will come of it. I think Jon was just a victim, plain and simple."

"You know what bugs me?" Bryers asked.

"What's that?"

"The abduction of Will Albrecht nineteen years ago. I think that's the wild card here."

"I feel the same way. Maybe we should cross reference the names of his known family and their friends with names from this current mess."

They made their way back upstairs, where Pamela was waiting with a Post-it note. She also held her cell phone in her hand. She was frowning at it when she handed the Post it with the address of Curtis Palmer on it.

"Here you go," she said.

"Are you okay, Mrs. Torrence?" Bryers asked.

"I suppose," she said. She then showed them her phone. Her Facebook app was opened and showing them a headline from what Mackenzie assumed was a local news outlet that someone on her timeline had shared. The headline read **Is There a Campground Killer in Strasburg?** A video was beneath it, but Mackenzie had no interest in viewing it. The headline was more than enough.

The media was getting into it deep now. That meant she had to work fast, to bring this case to a close before their currently quiet crime scene of a state park became a media circus.

"How confident are you that you'll find the man that did this to Jon?" Pamela asked.

"I can't give certainties," Mackenzie said.

Pamela nodded. "I understand that, I suppose. But if you could wrap it up before this makes national headlines and my son's face is all over TV, I'd appreciate it."

That was the closing comment as Mackenzie and Bryers made their exit. As they headed back to their car, Mackenzie paused for a moment to watch a van go cruising down the street. On the side, the call letters of a news station blared like a siren.

Mackenzie shook her head as they got into the car and drove in the same direction as the news van.

CHAPTER EIGHT

The address Pamela Torrence had given them led them to the outskirts of Strasburg. A few secondary roads took them away from the town and fed them out onto a series of county-maintained roads. These were unmarked roads with no lines along the center or sides, just strips of winding asphalt that led them deeper into the woods around the town. Along the way, Mackenzie took note of several locked gates on the side of the road, protecting what appeared to be dirt tracks that led back further into the woods. Most of these gates read **DO NOT ENTER! PROPERTY OF** and then named off one of several hunting clubs.

"Well, this certainly diminishes the charm of small-town life, doesn't it?" Bryers asked.

Mackenzie wasn't so sure. In the same way as the colors of the leaves in Little Hill State Park, this little rural excursion had also captured her attention. It was sort of like looking out to the ocean—the beauty and majesty of it was so great that it was sometimes easy to forget just how huge and ever-expanding it was.

"You okay?" Bryers asked her.

"Yeah," she said. "Just lost in my thoughts. How about you? You seem to be coming down with something."

"Oh, just some damn head cold or something. I don't catch them often but when I do, they're pretty bad."

Five minutes later, they reached what she assumed was a driveway. There were hints of gravel in it but it was mostly just dirt. The mailbox that sat on the other side of the road contained old spray-painted numbers, identifying the address as that of Curtis Palmer. The dirty driveway was short, coming to an end at a spot where it was hard to tell where the driveway ended and the dead grass of the lawn began. They pulled up next to the beaten up truck that was already parked there. A ramshackle house sat in front of them. It was in terrible need of a paint job and the porch looked like it might fall in if a strong breeze passed through. An old junked Ford pickup sat to the side of the property, along with several old rusted tools and a few discarded crumpled beer cans.

As Mackenzie and Bryers got out of the car, an old hunting dog came trotting around the side of the house. It looked almost malnourished and let out a sickly bark at the agents. It started sniffing the ground and then sat in a lazy heap under the edge of the porch.

"Now *this*," Mackenzie said, "diminishes the charm of small-town life."

"I'll say," Bryers said.

They walked toward the porch and the dog started barking again, now more like a pained howl. It apparently wasn't too concerned, though; it remained where it was, watching them with mild interest from his perch by the side of the porch.

Just as Mackenzie reached the first of the porch steps, the front door to the house opened. Curtis Palmer stepped out onto the porch, the human embodiment of his house. He was wearing a pair of tattered jeans with holes in both knees and nothing else. His chest looked concave in comparison to his rotund beer belly. His face was partially covered by scruff that could barely be called a beard. His mostly gray hair was sticking up wildly on his head and shagging down to nearly cover his eyes. He was holding a beer can in his left hand and the thumb of his right hand hitched into a belt loop on his jeans.

"Who the hell are you?" he asked.

It was not the best of welcomes and it nearly made Mackenzie point out that it was not quite noon yet and here he was, drinking from a can of beer. From the looks of the property and his beer belly, she doubted this was a rare occurrence.

Bryers apparently took offense to the way they were being greeted and perhaps even felt a little protective of Mackenzie. She assumed that was why he took one huge stride to stand in front of her and flash his badge to Curtis Palmer.

"I'm Agent Bryers and this is Agent White, with the FBI," he said. "We were hoping you could answer a few questions."

"FBI?" Curtis said, pronouncing the letters slowly. "You shitting me?"

"Not at all, sir," Bryers said.

Curtis made absolutely no effort to hide the fact that he was checking Mackenzie out. When he gave a lopsided grin when he was done, she took a step closer to the porch to compensate for the one Bryers had taken.

"No, we are not shitting you," Mackenzie said. "We were hoping you could answer some questions about the death of Jon Torrence."

"That's Ray's kid, right?" Curtis asked.

"That's right. You've heard about what happened, I assume?"

"I did," Curtis asked. "I feel sorry as hell for Ray and his wife. But I don't know why you'd waste your time coming to talk to me."

"We have it on good authority that you and Jon came to blows not too long ago," Mackenzie said.

"We did. But that doesn't mean I killed him."

"We're not suggesting that," Mackenzie said, hoping to try to find an opening for a civil conversation.

"So then what are you suggesting?" he asked, clearly trying to get a rise out of her. Mackenzie eyed him and she was pretty sure if she caught him staring at the shape of her breasts through her shirt and pantsuit, she was going to punch the bastard.

"We're merely suggesting that a man that came to blows with the young son of a hunting buddy *and* ended his marriage by beating on his wife and kid might be worth checking out in terms of our investigation."

"Go to hell," Curtis said. He gulped down a huge mouthful of beer, crumpled the can in his hand, and threw it down toward Mackenzie's feet.

"You understand that we can arrest you, correct?" Bryers asked.

"For what?"

"Failure to cooperate with an investigation," Bryers answered back.

Mackenzie knew this was a stretch, but doubted if Curtis Palmer did. He looked to them with a scowl before saying: "What do you need to know?"

"For starters," Mackenzie asked, "how often did you hunt with Jon and Ray Torrence?"

"I don't know. Maybe two or three times during deer season. I usually do my own thing. I only join the hunting club so I can hunt on certain people's land. I'm not a big fan of groups."

Huge surprise there, Mackenzie thought. But to dash that thought, she asked: "Do you recall what the argument was about that caused the fight between you and Jon?"

"Not really. But look…if you want me to be honest, I didn't like the kid. Sounds bad to say now that he's dead, but it's the truth. He was just irritating. Had no business out in the woods with a gun."

"And why not?" Mackenzie asked.

"He never paid attention. He was always distracted or trying to make jokes. I don't think the little shit ever bagged a single deer. He was just out there pretending. He said something to me one day—about me always drinking, I think. I took offense and threw a punch. Pretty sure you can't arrest me for that nine or ten months after it happened, now can you?"

48

"How well did you know Ray?" Bryers asked. "Did you like him any better than Jon?"

"Ray's an all right fella. Like I said, I'm sorry he lost his son but that ain't none of my concern."

"Do you ever spend any time in Little Hill State Park?" Bryers asked.

It was the look that Curtis gave them that made Mackenzie realize without a doubt that Curtis Palmer might be guilty of a lot of things, but the murder of Jon Torrence was not one of them.

"What for?" he asked. "There's some good land over there, but the fucking park rangers think they're GI Joe. No hunting. No trespassing. Useless land to me."

Mackenzie gave a nod and turned away. "Thank you for your time, Mr. Palmer," she said.

Curtis Palmer made a huffing sarcastic noise in response. Mackenzie didn't bother looking back to him a single time as she made her way to the car. As she opened the passenger side door, Bryers stepped close to her and eyed her with a bit of disappointment.

"That's it?" he asked.

"Yeah. He's scum, but he's not a killer. There's no way."

Bryers shrugged and looked back to the porch where Curtis had already gone back inside. "Yeah, I sort of agree. It was certainly worth checking out, though."

With that, Bryers got back behind the wheel of the car. When he cranked the engine to life, the old dog started howling again but did not see the point in getting to its feet. As Bryers backed out of the dirt driveway, Mackenzie pulled out her phone and selected a number she had recently programmed in.

The phone rang twice in her ear before it was answered.

"Hi, Sheriff Clements? It's Mackenzie White. I was wondering if you might have some time to speak."

"Yeah, I've got a few minutes. What can I do for you?"

"We were in town to speak with Pamela Torrence and thought we'd follow up on one of the files in the documents the state PD sent over late yesterday."

"Which file is that?" Clements asked.

"The apparent abduction of Will Albrecht," Mackenzie said. "We had planned on speaking to family members while we were here today only to find that there don't seem to be any."

"Yeah, that sounds about right," Clements said. "After Will went missing and the case sort of dead-ended, the Albrechts left town. Last I heard they were somewhere out in California with family on the father's side."

"How involved were the state police with that case?"

"Not too heavily," Clements said. "Only when the press started covering it. Keep in mind, though…I was pretty low in the ranks back then. I think I'd been a policeman for about two or three years when Will Albrecht went missing. I remember scant details, but nothing solid."

"And to your knowledge, he was never found?" Mackenzie asked. "Dead *or* alive?"

"Not that I know of."

"Do you think his disappearance might be linked to these killings in any way?"

"Probably not," he replied after some thought. "Why? Do you?"

"I have no idea," Mackenzie said. "But given the little bit I know about the case, it has to be considered."

"If you'll stick around for a few minutes, I'll make a call to records and see if I can get you everything we have on that. Come by the station in a bit and I'll see that you get them."

They ended the call and Mackenzie got the feeling that she might have won Clements over. Either that or he was just much more helpful and less irritating on the phone.

Outside, the afternoon wound down to evening as they headed over to the Strasburg PD in the hopes that a file from almost twenty years ago would reveal some answers to what the media was grossly calling the Campground Killer case.

CHAPTER NINE

Mackenzie felt like she was living in a rerun—almost like Bill Murray in *Groundhog Day*. It was reaching seven p.m. when Mackenzie finally made it home that night. While the drive to Strasburg wasn't really that long, the four hours of total driving time not only seemed like a waste, but it was also surprisingly draining.

She took only twenty minutes to shower, make a sandwich, and grab a beer before she opened up the file folder she had taken with her from the Strasburg PD. Clements had showed great pride in handing it over—almost like he was giving her the keys to some kingdom she was unaware of.

The folder contained more than twenty pages detailing the disappearance of Will Albrecht nineteen years ago. She'd gone over them in the car with Bryers at the wheel but had not been able to fully concentrate on them. She pored over them now, in the quiet solitude of her kitchen, eating her meager dinner and taking in the details of the case.

The material in the folder told a simple yet sad story.

Will Albrecht had gone missing at the age of seven. His parents had, at the time, lived half a mile from Little Hill State Park. Almost every weekend, they would take a walk down to the park and either hike, go fishing, or have a picnic. Once Will learned how to ride his bike, he would take it with them, pedaling down the paved trails and experimenting with his skill on the bumpier foot trails.

One day, when the Albrechts had gone to the park with plans for a picnic lunch and some fishing afterward, Will had gotten a little too far ahead of them on one of the footpaths. According to Mary Albrecht, Will had gone around a small curb that went down a hill. He was there one moment and then gone with a shout of joy as the bike took the hill. She called out to him once before Stan, her husband, had shook his head and said they should let him have some fun with it.

Twenty seconds later, when they got to the bottom of the hill Will had ridden down, Will was nowhere to be found. They scrambled ahead a few more feet (the police reports placed this distance as exactly eighty feet) before they found Will's bike. It had been upended, the handlebars turned almost completely around.

Their first worry was that he had lost control and been thrown from the bike. But a quick search of the wooded area around the trail turned up nothing. They searched fruitlessly for fifteen minutes before heading back to the welcome center to use their phone. It took twenty-five minutes for the first cop to arrive. Within an hour, five more had arrived.

Within eight hours, there was a town-wide search for Will Albrecht.

His body was never found and although the investigation went on for the better part of a year, not a shred of evidence was ever found to suggest what might have happened. No traces of blood or foul play. No traces that he had wrecked, banged his head, and simply went wandering out into the woods. By all accounts and purposes, Will Albrecht had simply disappeared.

There was nothing in the reports that Mackenzie could use other than the names of the officers that had led the charge on the case. She had copied these down and planned to use them if she continued to feel as if the abduction was somehow related to the murders.

She tried her best to place herself in the position of someone that would not only abduct a kid and but also kill people, butcher them significantly, and then scatter the remains in a state park. To dump the remains on government property was a ballsy move. It further reinforced her theory that the killer knew the area well—a local or someone with an almost intimate knowledge of the park.

Twenty seconds, she thought. *That's all it took for the abductor to snatch up Will and get far enough way into the woods to conceal himself.*

Something about that scenario unnerved her. Twenty seconds…that spoke of planning, knowing exactly where to grab Will, and how to get away without so much as a noise.

It made her think that they were not looking for just any killer. They were looking for someone that took the time to plan and was smarter than the average criminal.

It also made her think that if Will Albrecht *was* someone linked to the more recent murders, he was dead. He had probably died within a few hours of being abducted. Mackenzie wondered if bits of his body had remained in the forest, somewhere outside of the search perimeters. She wondered if his bones were still out there, cleaned of flesh and muscle by woodland animals.

It was a morbid way to think, but if she was going to get into the mind of a killer this severe, her thoughts were going to have to take something of a twist. To sever fingers, heads, and legs…it spoke of some sort of mental imbalance but also patience and determination.

She tried to come up with a quick profile in her head. Probably a male. Not very strong physically but quite rigid in terms of mental stamina. So far there seemed to be no connection between Jon Torrence and Marjorie Leinhart, so the killer might be selecting victims at random. The only link she could see was Little Hill State Park—and that was a pretty wide target.

With a heavy sigh, she pushed herself away from her kitchen table. After reading through the material for over an hour, trying to find something of substance, she realized that it was getting late but she was not tired at all. If anything, she seemed to have an extra bit of adrenaline still surging.

She needed to step away from the paperwork for a while. She needed to give her mind a break. She needed to tap into something normal. She was quickly coming to understand that she had to put forth extra effort to make sure she remembered that she *did* have something of a regular life behind the veil of her identity as an agent. Of course, some of that life of normalcy was connected to the FBI.

And while part of her wanted to call Harry and ask him out for a drink, she opted against it. She didn't want to further confuse him and she certainly didn't want to get derailed from the case with his endless questions and not-so-subtle subtleties about how badly he wanted to sleep with her.

So she flipped on the TV and checked the local and national news. She sat in front of the TV for an hour, flipping through the news channels, and was relieved to find that she didn't see any mention of the Campground Killer. She wondered, though, if that might be different in the morning. She knew the media acted quickly and bad news tended to spread faster than good.

With the sense of being pushed by a clock she could not see, she finally made herself go to bed. When she closed her eyes, she saw the woods in Little Hill State Park. She pictured a young boy riding his bike around a curb and then imagined the blank space of twenty seconds from a parent's perspective.

It was that harrowing image that settled into her mind as she gradually fell asleep.

***

Mackenzie was standing in a large open field. The grass swayed like the sea, coming up to her seven-year-old knees. Her parents were sitting beside her in the grass. Her father was slowly unspooling a kite that seemed to swim in the wind over their heads.

It was high up there, so high that Mackenzie thought it could actually touch the sun.

"Can it go higher, Daddy?" she asked with a giggle.

"I don't know, Mac," he said. "We're just about out of string. But you can come over here and hold it if you want."

She nodded and dashed over to her father. She took the spool and grinned at the feeling of the wind pulling the kite. She started giggling wildly.

"Look, Daddy! I'm doing it!"

She started to dance around and when she did, the spool dropped from her hands. It went rolling through the high grass, the kite pulling it as the wind started to carry it away, uncontrolled.

"Whoops!"

Still giggling, she chased after it. When she reached it and placed a hand down, though, she was in such a panic over losing the kite that she nearly stepped on the rabbit that was splayed out in the grass.

She let out of a little squeal and leaped back.

"What is it?" her dad asked. Her mother was right behind him, worried about her squealing.

The three of them stared down at the rabbit. It was small but not quite a baby. A huge gash occupied the area where its stomach should have been, Blood and muscle showed through. The grass around it was stained with blood. It twitched its back legs uselessly and stared in frozen fright up at the three humans.

"What's wrong with it?" Mackenzie asked.

"Oh, honey..." her mom said.

"It looks like another animal got it. Maybe a fox."

"Gross," Mackenzie said. She then looked closer at the rabbit. "It's hurting, isn't it?"

"Yes, it looks like it." He seemed to think hard about something and then said, "Maybe you should turn away, kiddo. I can help it."

"How?"

Her mother put an arm around her and turned her away. "Come on," she said. "Let's go get the kite."

Mackenzie nodded and started to walk away from her father and the dead rabbit. Still, she heard the crack as something broke. Later on in life, she understood that this had been her father breaking its neck, putting it out of its misery.

As her mother led her through the field, toward a kite that would in real life get away from them and get tangled in a tree, she

54

saw Bryers standing in the field. He was coughing heavily and looked ghostly pale.

"That's called a mercy killing," Bryers said between coughs.

She turned back to where her father stood and saw that he was holding the rabbit in hands. He approached slowly, offering the corpse to her.

She screamed then, a scream that tore through the dream and into the waking world where Mackenzie jerked awake, still screaming.

Mackenzie sat there, breathing hard. She didn't bother trying to go back to sleep. She could not remember ever having such a terrible nightmare before. Like the usual dream she had of her father dead on his bed, this dream had also taken a memory from her childhood and used it for its base. The scene in the field had actually happened when she was seven years old. Everything in the dream had been accurate up until the moment after she'd heard the cracking of the rabbit's neck.

Everything else had simply been fuel from the nightmare.

She did find herself thinking of that damned rabbit from time to time. It had crept into her dreams for a while as a child, and on the nights where the dreams truly haunted her, she would wake up, certain there was a mostly dead rabbit limping across her bedroom floor.

When she slid out of bed and headed back to the kitchen to look over the notes again, it was 4:45. She put on some coffee, fried a few eggs, and went to work.

To wake herself up, she started jotting down details of the case on a notepad. It was an exercise she'd used ever since middle school, a way to memorize things and unlock the meaning that might be hiding in the simplest of problems.

Jon Torrence—left leg, right hand (still missing)

Marjorie Leinhart—right leg and all fingers (never found), attempted beheading

Will Albrecht – abducted from trail, never found

Jon: runner. Marjorie: ?? Will: bike

She wanted to rule out Will Albrecht's disappearance. It didn't seem to fit. If the kid had been the earliest victim of this killer, why had the body not been dumped like the others?

It was an impossible question to answer but what she *did* know was that something about the unresolved nature of the abduction seemed to *make* it fit into the current case. And for now, she wasn't prepared to eliminate any possible links.

She then got out the color map of the park that Smith had provided her with. She made little marks at each of the sites where bodies had been discovered. As she placed the marks on the map, she thought about the terrible stories Charlie Holt and Joe Andrews had told her—how rangers sometimes had to undergo terrible situations without proper training. It made her look at the map with a whole new perspective as she tried to make sense of the pen points she had placed on the map.

After half an hour of this, Mackenzie poured herself a cup of black coffee. The restless fear still lurking in her heart from the nightmare, she was prepared to do whatever it took to find some answers.

With her coffee in hand, she went to her couch and put on the TV. Within ten minutes, she saw a headline about the Campground Killer. It was on the local news but had not yet gotten any attention in the national media. Still...this was bad.

She gulped down her coffee, readied herself for the day, and hurried in to work. She knew she was working against the clock—and if they didn't solve this case soon, it would get too big for all of them.

CHAPTER TEN

Miranda Peters was pissed off.

She was sweating, her arms were covered in mosquito bites, and one of the right legs of her telescope was busted. More than that, Cho Liu, her lab partner, was going to be very late. She'd texted about two hours ago. At least she'd been honest.

Sorry. Tony came by. Need a good lay before coming to the woods. See you around 10:30.

It was 10:37 now. Miranda was fully prepared for Tony to come tagging along with Cho. Miranda couldn't imagine walking through these creepy woods at night by herself. It had taken enough nerve for her to do it in the thinning light of the afternoon five hours ago. She'd been carrying the telescope in its case, as well as her book bag and laptop case. Cho was going to have the same sort of load and Miranda didn't envy her at all. That was going to be a brutal walk in the dark, even with a headlamp.

She looked up to the moon through the telescope. She had managed to brace the busted leg with a small piece of wood and was pretty proud of the job she'd done. She focused the lens until she could make out the clear definition of the Byrgius crater and then slowly adjusted the telescope's position to the east. In about an hour, she'd be able to see Venus quite clearly. Cho had the camera they would need and if she didn't show up, this whole trip would be a bust.

Not that it mattered. She was an English major and this astronomy class was just filler. It had been fun and, if she was honest, she'd been excited about the idea of a camping trip to catch Venus in its crescent phase. The instructor had offered every student the chance for extra credit through observing different astronomical events. Miranda and Cho had chosen to try capturing the phenomenon known as Venus's Ashen Light.

But none of that would matter if Cho didn't get her ass here *very* soon. Miranda had an okay-at-best telescope, so it would take the lenses on Cho's telescopic camera to capture the Ashen Light when it came into view in fifty-four minutes.

Peering into the darkness through the scope, Miranda heard footsteps approaching from below the slight hill she had set up her tent and telescope on. Her heart sighed with relief. She never *really* thought Cho would let her down. They weren't exactly best friends or anything, but Cho was very reliable.

As the footsteps got closer, coming through the slight brush that broke off of the trail and up the hill Miranda and Cho had selected last week, Miranda looked away from the telescope.

"It's about time," Miranda said. "Damn, girl...I hope you rocked his world because you had me worried."

Cho said nothing. And it was that initial silence that spooked Miranda for the first time. Cho was a chatterbox; she would have probably been talking right away, the moment she saw the small glow of Miranda's battery-operated lantern light.

"Cho?"

Still no answer. But the footsteps kept coming closer and closer. Through the trees and the cruel darkness of night, Miranda started to see a figure emerging. It was then that she realized just how deep her trouble could become if this was not Cho. She was easily four miles away from the nearest road and a quarter of a mile away from the nearest trail. She was also nearly two hours away from college. Put that all together and she was basically stranded. And alone.

"Cho...if this is some sort of prank, it's not funny."

But the figure stepped out of the forest and the glow from her lantern revealed that this was not Cho. It was a man—about six feet tall and with facial features that seemed to swim in the shadows her lantern created.

"Who are you?" Miranda asked.

"Just a lover of nature," the man said as he advanced toward her.

"My boyfriend is just over that way," Miranda lied, pointing to a thicket of bushes and trees to the right.

The man only smiled and came closer. Miranda backed up, knocking the telescope over.

"I have a gun," she said, knowing the threat sounded thin. She *did* have a knife, but it was tucked away in one of the bags in her tent.

The man only chuckled. In the darkness, it was the most menacing thing Miranda had ever heard. Fear spiked through her heart and her legs froze. Should she retreat into the woods? Should she go for the knife?

The man dashed toward her with uncanny speed. He kicked over the battery-operated lantern as Miranda raced for the tent. She felt his hands on her leg, gripping it tight and pulling her out of the tent and toward him. She opened her mouth to scream but the sound was blocked when he placed a hand over her mouth.

Again, she tried to scream but she only felt the vibrations of it through the hand cupped over her mouth. She felt herself lifted into the air as the world seemed to spin around her and then she was hauled over his shoulder. He was not very big but seemed to possess brute strength. She fought and fought and all she got for her efforts was a clubbing blow from his left hand that struck her directly in the forehead.

The world went darker than the night around her. Before she slipped into unconsciousness, she watched the little flickering light from her lantern grow dimmer and dimmer as the stranger carried her deeper into the forest.

CHAPTER ELEVEN

Even when she'd been nothing more than a patrol cop working the sleepy highways of Nebraska, Mackenzie had not liked to waste her time with leads that she *knew* would come to nothing. And while she felt her current lead was flimsy at best, she also knew that small inconsequential leads could often lead to productive thinking that opened up other opportunities.

That's what she hoped would happen with this current lead as Bryers pulled their car into the lot of a sloppy-looking garage called Strasburg Car Care. She could tell by the look on Bryers's face that he also thought this was a waste of time. But simply being back in Strasburg seemed to pacify McGrath and as long as he was not breathing down their necks, Mackenzie was happy.

A tenuous connection was what had brought them to Strasburg Car Care. While there had been no surviving local family to speak with about Will Albrecht's disappearance, Mackenzie had been able to dig up the name of a close childhood friend. That friend had a rap sheet with a few DUIs and unpaid parking tickets, but nothing too serious. His name was Andy Vaughan, employee of Strasburg car Care since he had started working at the age of fifteen.

When Mackenzie stepped through the garage doors, she saw her man right away. His identity was given away by the nametag over the breast pocket of his work uniform: ANDY. Currently, he was changing the oil on a truck that was easily thirty years old. When he saw Mackenzie and Bryers, he rolled his eyes.

"Customers aren't allowed in the garage," he said, clearly annoyed.

"We're not customers," Mackenzie said, flashing her badge.

"Oh," he said, his eyes going wide at the sight of her badge. "One second then, if you don't mind."

"Take your time."

While they waited for Andy Vaughan to finish up, she and Bryers looked around the garage. Apparently, Andy was the only one working. And from the looks of the place, she figured a single employee per shift might be as much as Strasburg Car Care could afford.

A few minutes later, Andy stepped out of the garage and waved them into the small office attached to the garage. "Sorry about that," he said as he took a seat on a stool behind the counter. He wiped his hands on a shop rag and said, "What can I help you with?"

"I'm Agent White and this is Agent Bryers. I know it may seem like it's coming out of left field, but we had a few questions about Will Albrecht."

He looked very confused at first and then a look of sadness came across his face. Something about the unexpected sorrow made him look much older than his twenty-six years. "Wow," he said. "Okay. I'll try to help but, man...I haven't even thought of Will in years."

"We believe his disappearance could be linked to a recent case," Mackenzie said. "So if you think hard on it, what can you tell us about what you remember about Will, the disappearance, and his family?"

"Are you talking about the Campground Killer?" he asked. "How on earth is *that* linked?"

"There is no clear link," Mackenzie said, quickly dodging the question. "So, if you could please just focus on the question..."

"Sure," Andy said. "Well, if I can be frank, his family sucks. I know people deal with grief in their own ways and all, but they were just jerks afterwards. They wanted help from no one. They moved, you know? I'm not sure where, but not even a year after he disappeared, they up and moved. Seemed weird as hell to me."

It had seemed odd to Mackenzie as well but the records indicated that the family had been more than helpful with answering questions about the disappearance in the years that followed. They'd simply wanted to distance themselves from the community after their son had gone missing. Mackenzie understood it but also felt that it *had* been a little suspicious.

"I know it seems like forever ago," Mackenzie said, "but can you think of anyone that might have wanted to hurt Will or his family?"

"Not at all," Andy said. "Will was a cool kid, you know? And in a town like this, there are really no enemies...even when kids don't get along in school, their parents would get together over beers and sort it out. It's always been like that around here."

"Did you ever hang out with Will and his family?" Mackenzie asked. "Playdates, sleepovers, anything like that?"

"Oh yeah, sure. We used to ride bikes all the time. Usually just around his house. Sometimes at the park, but that ended for me after Will went missing, my mom sort of lost her mind after that. She never let me do much of anything after Will disappeared."

"And at the park, do you ever remember Will getting into any altercations? Were there ever any suspicious characters back then, hanging out at the park?"

"Not that I remember," he said. "Later, when I got to high school, some kids went out there to drink and smoke pot every now and then. I do remember there being a few instances of the cops having to break tough on homeless people ambling through and bothering people every now and then. Asking for spare change and stuff, you know?"

Mackenzie thought that might be worth looking into but at the same time, she felt that Will Albrecht's disappearance might be a dead end. It was starting to feel less and less related to the deaths of Jon Torrence and Marjorie Leinhart.

She was searching for any other follow-up questions to make this trip worth it when her cell phone rang. She didn't recognize the number on the display as she answered, but it had a Strasburg area code.

"This is Agent White," she said.

"Agent White, this is Sheriff Clements. You and your partner might want to get back out here."

"Oh yeah? We're in Strasburg right now," she said. "What's up?"

"Well, we've got another body on our hands. And this one is *fresh*."

CHAPTER TWELVE

This time, Clements didn't meet them with a golf cart. Instead, he had an ATV waiting for them behind the visitor's center. Neither Mackenzie nor Bryers had ever driven one but Mackenzie figured it couldn't be so hard. She gladly took the driver's position, gripping the handlebars with a slight stir of excitement. With Bryers clinging on to the back bars, she steered them out down the central path and stopped when they came to two other carts blocking any further progress.

One of Clements's deputies was sitting at this makeshift roadblock. Mackenzie remembered his face from their first venture out into Little Hill. He gave them only the faintest of nods as a salutation.

"Follow me, please," was all he said.

Without another word, the officer led them into the woods. They were led in a totally different direction this time, headed directly to the east of the last crime scene. It instantly made Mackenzie more aware that the killer *had* to know these forests well. *Almost as well as a park ranger,* she thought with suspicion.

They had been walking for five minutes when Mackenzie started to hear arguing voices from up ahead. It was much the same as it had been at the first crime scene in Little Hill State Park. It irritated her to no end; these men were too worried about who held the most sway out here rather than trying to find the killer. In front of her, even the officer that was leading them let out a sigh, making it clear that he thought it was stupid, too.

As they drew closer, Mackenzie could make out all of what was being said. She followed behind the officer but, at that point, was really just following the voices of dissention further up ahead.

"—and if you have a problem with it, you can call my chief!"

"Fuck your chief! If you have issues with *me* being out here, you can call the governor!"

"He wouldn't get off his ass to answer the phone!"

"Back up, would you, you're too close to the *evidence*!"

"Don't tell me how to do my job!"

Finally, Mackenzie started to see the men. There were only five of them today: Clements, Smith, and three park rangers. She recognized one of the park rangers as Charlie Holt, the man with the weird acorn obsession. His partner, Joe Andrews, was also there. They were all standing very close together in what looked like the moments before a nasty playground-type brawl.

63

"Gentlemen," she said loudly. "Can we keep it together, please?"

"Watch your tone," Clements said.

"Same goes for you," Bryers said, stepping forward. "Could you please *all* show some respect to the deceased and act like grown men?"

Everyone fell quiet again as their attention was drawn back to the reason they were all gathered there.

Mackenzie took it all in but had to focus fairly hard. It was…well, it was *bad.* It was easily the worst condition she had ever seen a body in. The fact that it was indeed very fresh as Clements had said on the phone made it that much worse. The others managed to keep quiet and stay a respectful distance away while she and Bryers took it in.

"My God," Bryers said.

Mackenzie only nodded. The head had been severed from the body but didn't look too much like a human head. What Mackenzie was seeing made her think of what a pumpkin looks like after it has been tossed away after Halloween. The sight was almost too gruesome to make sense of so she turned her attention to the body, sprawled about twenty feet away from the smashed head.

The state of the body wasn't much better. There were large bruises everywhere. From what Mackenzie could tell, the entire chest seemed to be caved in. The left arm was also in a bad state, as the shoulder had not only been dislocated but nearly removed from the body altogether. Mackenzie was fairly certain that an autopsy would reveal that the shoulder had been pulverized. There were also several deep gouge marks in the buttocks and the right leg had clearly been broken; the knee was in the same sort of shape as the busted shoulder.

"Who found the body?" he asked.

"We did," Smith said. "We got a call this morning from a James Madison University student. She said her friend had gone missing—that she had been camping in these woods last night. We were already on the way over here with a drone, hoping to use it to surveil the area. We sent it up right away and found the body within half an hour."

"Did you find her campsite?"

"We did," Charlie Holt said. "We haven't made it over there yet, though. We literally just got here fifteen minutes ago."

"Did the girl that called have anything useful?"

"No," Smith said. "We haven't called her yet."

"With all due respect," Clements said, "the iron is hot. I think we need to strike."

"Strike what?" Mackenzie asked. "Without leads, there's no striking."

"Well, it's your show," Smith said. "I'll gladly pass over the power to you on this." He looked over to the three park rangers, one of whom looked like he might puke at any moment. "Anyone got a problem with that?"

All three of them shook their heads.

"Thank you," Mackenzie said. She looked to Bryers for approval and he gave it with a thin smile and a nod.

"Okay. Rangers…have you already given the instruction to shut the park down?"

"Yes," said Andrews.

"And how many men can you get on shift today?"

"As many as six," Holt said.

"Get all six of them," she said. "Station them at whatever secondary or maintenance roads you have coming in and out of the park. How many are there?"

"Three," answered Holt.

"That's perfect, then. Have them stationed at those roads, making sure no one gets in or out without the proper ID. How soon can you make that happen?"

All three of the park rangers seemed to step up in that moment. Given a specific instruction that they were in charge of apparently snapped them out of whatever funk they'd had brewing between the local and state PD. Still, she wasn't quite sure as to how skilled they would be.

"They'll be stationed at the entrances within twenty minutes," Andrews said, pulling out his phone.

"I need someone to be the point man for the rangers," Mackenzie said. "Who wants that duty?"

"That would be me," Andrews said. Mackenzie noticed that Charlie Holt sort of rolled his eyes behind Andrews when he volunteered.

"Good," she said. "I need you to come up with a list of potential sites that someone could potentially live for several days within the park and not be seen."

"I doubt there are places like that," Andrews said. "There's the few maintenance sheds but that's it."

"And those are under twenty-four-hour surveillance," Charlie Holt added.

"Keep in mind, Agent White," Andrews said, "the farther away from the main trails you go, the thicker the terrain gets. We're talking briars, thickets, things like that. But I'll get you a list of sites."

She then looked to Smith and found it was harder to give him orders, as he had been the only one to really show her respect this entire time. "Officer Smith, I need you to get on the phone with the student that called the missing person report in. Do we know who the victim is?"

"Miranda Peters. Nineteen years old. An English major at JMU. The friend is Cho Liu. She was supposed to meet her here last night for some astronomy project. Cho got here about two hours late and when she arrived, Miranda was nowhere to be found."

"Can you break the news to her and see what she can tell you?"

"Can do," he said with a frown.

"Clements," she said, "since the park is within your jurisdiction, I need you with us. Can you take us to the campsite? Andrews, I need you with us, please."

"Yeah, gladly," he said, taking one last look at the grisly sight before him.

"Everyone good?" Mackenzie asked.

She got a series of nods, and a smile from Bryers.

"Call me the moment anything of note pops up," she said. "Clements was right: the iron *is* hot. Let's find something to strike out and nail this sonofabitch before an entire nation of news crews makes it that much harder for us."

***

The campsite was about two miles away from where the body had been dumped. It required them to get on the ATV again, going around the roadblock and deeper into the park. It took them ten minutes of riding on the cart and another eight minutes of walking to reach it. Clements led the way through the forest, looking to the screenshot from the drone for reference to make sure they were on the right track. Mackenzie, Bryers, and Andrews followed behind him.

"This makes no sense," Mackenzie said. "The body this morning was fresh. Two hours…three at most, right? So how is he getting around without a car or anything with wheels? Even if he has an ATV or something, there would be tire tracks somewhere."

"Not to mention that we'd hear an ATV running through here," Andrews said.

"It has to be someone within the park," Mackenzie said. "Andrews, given the size and shape of the park, what are the chances that someone could have dumped the body in that location two hours ago and then made it out of the park's borders?"

"It's possible," he said. "But they'd have to really be hauling ass."

Mackenzie thought about this for a moment. She knew that if they yielded no results in the next few days, the local PD and maybe even the FBI would have several men out in the forests, scouring the land inch by inch. She wondered idly how many more would have to die before the State flew in a helicopter rather than offering up a drone.

The idea that the killer could still be within the park was infuriating. It made Mackenzie move with urgent speed, her thoughts racing just as fast as her feet.

When they finally arrived to the campsite, Mackenzie's sense of urgency only increased. The campsite was small and desolate looking. A single tent had been pitched, a single-sleeper that had been staked into the ground without much thought or expertise. A little battery-operated lantern had been kicked over, still shining uselessly in the afternoon sunlight. A telescope was knocked over at the edge of the small clearing.

Mackenzie picked up a stick from the ground and walked over to the tent. The entrance flap was unzipped, allowing her to push the flap back with the stick so she did not taint the scene with her fingerprints. Inside, there wasn't much to see: a pillow, a sleeping bag, and a single backpack. From what she could tell, nothing had been gone through. The killer had not been interested in theft; he'd just wanted Miranda Peters.

She crawled out of the tent and saw Bryers and Clements scouring the ground. She noticed that Bryers had hunkered down to a knee and was looking closely at a particular section of ground.

"Find something?" she asked.

"I don't know," he said. He pointed to an area that went downhill—back toward the small rise in the ground they had come up. The foliage and dirt on the ground wasn't necessarily messy but there did seem to be a disturbance of sorts. But that wasn't what Bryers was pointing at.

"Is it just me trying to stretch?" he said. "Or is that part of a shoeprint?"

He was right. It *was* a print. It was only a partial print, but it was there in the dirt. And to be so noticeable, it had to have been recent. She studied it closely, taking down every mental note she could about it.

She knew right away that this was not Miranda Peters's print. From the look of her body, she had weighed around one thirty, one forty at most. But this shoeprint was large. She figured it was at least a size 11. The pattern of the underside as well as the shape of it also indicated that it was likely a work boot of some kind.

"What have we got?" Clements asked, walking over and clearly not wanting to be left out.

"A potential shoeprint from the killer," Mackenzie said. "A work boot, from the looks of it." She got to her feet and looked in the direction the print seemed to have been coming from. She pointed behind them and slightly to the right. "It looks like he was coming from that direction. Is there anything back there?"

"Just trees and more trees," Clements said. "I'd say the park grounds go on another twenty miles or so in that direction. One of the maintenance roads cuts through for a bit at some point, but that's it."

"Maintenance for what?" Bryers asked.

"That particular road connects the visitor's center to the electrical shed," Andrews said. "That's where the breakers for the light posts and spotlights along the river are."

"Any security cameras out at that shed?" Mackenzie asked.

"None, unlike the sheds that hold ATVs, chemicals, and so on."

She snapped a picture of the shoe print with her phone and took one last look around the site. "Clements, can you get some men out here quickly to dust the area for prints? The tent, the telescope, the lantern...everything."

"Absolutely," he said. "Anything else?"

"Yes. Work with Smith to work out a schedule to have the drone flying over the park. Keep an eye out for oddities of any kind...no matter how small. Do you have the manpower to keep men checking out the footage?"

"We do."

"Great. And please keep me posted."

They left the campsite and headed back for the golf cart. Mackenzie tried her hardest to organize everything that needed to be done, making lists within her head. But much to her dismay, she kept getting sidetracked by flashes of Miranda Peters—her head severed and mashed in, her body beaten and broken.

She often found herself wanting to get into the head of the killers she chased down. It helped her to understand their motives and how they worked. But this time, she was struggling to put an

MO together. The man clearly *wanted* to be found…it was evident by the way he was dumping the bodies. But perhaps he saw some sort of sport to it…trying to see how long he could keep it up before he was caught.

That meant that the killer was working with the impression that he had nothing to lose; even if he was apprehended, he would not care. And that made him incredibly dangerous. There was no clear direction, no reasoning at all.

This time, the idea of trying to get into a killer's head seemed a little too much. How was she supposed to understand the brutality and disrespect for human life on a level like she had seen with Miranda Peters?

Stepping into a mind like that would be frightening. For the first time in her career, Mackenzie wondered if this case was too dark and warped for her to fully grasp.

CHAPTER THIRTEEN

He listened to the screams of the woman he had taken from the campsite as he sipped from a Mason jar of moonshine. He was watching the sun come up from his ramshackle front porch. The trees blocked most of the sunrise but the light that *did* make it through was pristine and golden. It made the woods seem to come alive.

This woman was a little different from the others he had taken. This one had some fight in her. She had come to before he had gotten her back to his cabin. He'd had to hit her again using the handle from an axe he had lost the blade to some time ago. And then when he had dumped her into the hole in the ground—nothing but a shallow grave, really—and covered it with the thick sheets of plywood—her screams had been defiant rather than pleas for help.

So far, all of his victims had begged for their life. They'd offered him money, or sex, or just about anything he could imagine. But not this one. She'd told him that when she got free, she'd slit his throat. She'd cut off his dick. She'd break his legs and torture him.

Of course, those defiant screams had only lasted for an hour or so. After that, they had become plain old screams—screams she probably hoped would go traveling through the woods and fall on helpful ears. And now her screams were hoarse and desperate. Soon, she'd barely be able to speak, much less scream.

He knew none of her screams were doing any good. He was far enough out in the forest where her screams would not be heard. And just in case, the enclosed hole in the earth, topped off by the thick plywood sheets, kept her screams trapped in the earth, only slipping through into the air as a series of sad little vibrations.

With the pleasant burn of moonshine in his stomach and the warmth of the morning sun on his face, he left the porch and walked back inside his little cabin. It was a tiny little shack of a place, completely off the grid. He did not own a computer, a TV, a phone. He had given up on electric lights about five years ago, realizing that it was just stupid to pay some of the little money he had for electricity he rarely even used.

The shack consisted of three rooms: a small living area, his bedroom (which was kept meticulously cleaned) and the room he referred to as his study. The study was the largest of the three rooms but did not have wooden floors like the others. This floor was made of dirt. He stepped onto the hard-packed earth floor as the screams and moans of the girl with the telescope started to become raspy mewling sounds.

She had started kicking at the plywood sheets now. This would be just as effective as her screams. The plywood was tied to sturdy wooden poles that stood to each side of his study. Even if the girl could slam her full weight into the sheets, they'd not move an inch. One end of each rope was tied to the wooden poles and the other end was threaded through two holes, one in the top and one at the bottom of the plywood sheets.

He stood in the doorway of the room, closed his eyes, and listened to her. She was getting close to giving up now. Still, he thought she was special. He thought he might keep her for a while. Maybe for a very long time. He'd done it before and it had turned out to be a truly rewarding experience.

As he peered into his study, he heard something behind him. It had come from the living area, a noise he was used to and constantly irritated him.

"What is it now?" he asked.

He listened closely, shaking his head and biting back the venom and anger that tried to come to the surface.

"Are you fucking kidding me?" he asked, almost shouting. He still held his jar of moonshine and nearly threw it into the living room. "No. It's not even something to think about!"

He listened again, the reply making him even angrier.

"After everything you've seen? Are you serious? Have you lost your fucking mind?" He then let the venom out in a roar of rage. It hurt his throat and negated the good feelings that the moonshine had started to create. Rather than throw the jar across the cabin, he took a large mouthful of it, nearly gagging on it as he swallowed it.

In the midst of coughing, he yelled into the living area. "Get out! Get out of my sight before I kill you!"

He was breathing hard, getting a stabbing pain in his stomach. He carefully set the jar of moonshine down, knowing that his supply was running low.

With his screaming conversation over and the living area in silence again, he turned back to his study. The woman under the plywood had gone quiet. She'd heard the whole thing, no doubt. She'd heard the argument and had heard him lose his temper. If he planned on keeping her around for a while, he probably needed to explain himself.

With a sigh, he entered the study. He walked to the plywood sheets on the dirt floor, appreciating the rest of the room. There was a small bench that contained a pair of pliers, a hammer, two large butcher knives, a paring knife, and several empty jars. Several hooks hung from the walls. One of them held the hide of a doe. Two others held handsaws, one very large and one quite small. A sledgehammer was propped in the far corner, the mallet end stained with blood from some dark time in the past that he could barely remember.

He knelt by the plywood, doing everything he could to push the rage he'd just felt aside. Nothing good came from it. He knew this, but sometimes it was so hard to understand this. He placed his hand on the top sheet of plywood and cleared his throat, wanting to sound as friendly as he could.

"I'm sorry you had to hear that," he said.

The woman made a soft choking noise in response.

"Look. I'm going to let you out. I think you and I need to talk. I know you're scared. But I'm done hurting you. I want to take care of you. So…I'm going to let you out. If you try to run, I'll *have* to hurt you and I really don't want to. Okay?"

The woman said nothing. He could picture her trembling down in that little hole. Maybe she was paralyzed with the hope that she was going to be freed. He would give her that. He would give her a new life. He could redeem her, could make her something new.

Anxious now, he untied the ropes from the wooden posts. When both ropes were curled on the floor, he grabbed the plywood sheets by the edges. The two sheets were bolted together and quite heavy but he was able to slide them away without much trouble.

He looked into the hole and regarded the girl. Her hands were tied with rope at her wrists. Another strand of rope was tied just above her knees. The hole was only three feet deep but he always thought it looked so much deeper when there was someone in it. Her eyes were wide with fear and she was shaking from head to toe. In that moment, he felt like God. Her fate was in his hands. He knew it, she knew it, and it bonded them.

He got down onto his knees, reached in, and grabbed the strand of rope that bound her wrists. He hauled her to her knees and then did his best to help her to her feet. She was weeping and cringing at his touch as he guided her to the lip of the dirt hole.

"Now don't be like that," he said as he helped her get her weight positioned properly to pull herself from the hole.

She gasped, letting out a huge sob. She was absolutely terrified.

"It's okay," he said as she got her first knee out onto the dirt floor of the study. "Really, I only want to—"

In a sudden movement that confused him more than alarmed him, the girl came rocketing off of the ground. She propelled herself upward, kicking out of the hole with her left foot and pushing off of the ground with her right knee. She rocketed into the air and although she did not go very high at all, it did the job.

The top of her head connected solidly with the underside of his jaw. There was a musical *click* in the study as her skull met his chin and his teeth clinked together. He cried out in surprise and fell backward. He fell into the small bench, sending its contents to the ground. By the time he hit the ground and realized just what had happened, the woman was making her way out of the study in an odd sort of hopping motion—all she was able to do with the way her legs were tied together above the knee.

She nearly fell down but slammed into the doorframe. She hit it with such force that the entire cabin shook.

And just like that, all of his rage returned. It came spiraling up in him like a nest of angry bees, demanding someone be stung. He let out a bellow of absolute hatred as he scrambled back to his feet. As he did so, he reached out and grabbed the old stained sledgehammer. As he hefted it up and started forward, he could hear the woman crashing through the living area, headed for the porch.

Anger flashed through him and seemed to propel him forward. He was barely aware that he was even moving. Everything was a blur of red, edged by a razor-sharp definition that he had long ago learned came with the most acute sort of rage.

He saw her as she dashed onto the porch, still in that peculiar hopping stride. He was drawing closer—five steps away, then four. At three, he was nearly at the door, nearly blinded by the sunlight that now seemed to have set the forest on fire.

In front of him, the woman hopped off of the porch. Her feet landed awkwardly and she went down, sprawling forward.

A grin came to his face, like a deep cut across his head. He stepped out onto the porch and tossed the sledgehammer over his shoulder.

He stepped onto the ground just as she tried scrambling to her feet. She looked like a wounded fawn, too dumb to realize it was already dead.

She opened her mouth to scream just as he brought the sledgehammer down.

Her scream never found the air but the sound of the blow, although rather wet and muted, sent a bevy of nearby birds into the air.

CHAPTER FOURTEEN

When Mackenzie and Bryers reached the parking lot and headed for their car, she saw that Smith was on his cell phone. He leaning against his car and speaking in hushed, apologetic tones. Without even hearing a word, Mackenzie was fairly certain that he was speaking with the parents of Miranda Peters.

When he ended the call, he hurried over to Mackenzie. He looked profoundly sad, like delivering the news had broken his heart a bit.

"Thanks for handling that," Mackenzie said.

"Sure," he said. "I think it might help if someone heads over there and speaks with them."

"Where do they live?"

"Moorefield, West Virginia. About an hour and fifteen minutes from here."

Mackenzie and Bryers shared a look over the hood of the car. Bryers gave a nod and a shrug and then stepped into the car.

"We'll do it. I just need you to please help Clements any way you can. I've already asked him to work with you on doing some fly-overs with your drone. He'll fill you in."

"Sounds good. And look…thanks for pulling this all together. I thought we were going to come to blows out there."

"It sometimes pays to be the only girl in a bar fight," she said with a smile. He returned it in a way that made her think he might like to take her out to a bar—sans the fight.

"You kicked everyone's ass into gear. The park rangers are blocking off all of the maintenance and secondary roads into the park as we speak. Cho Liu has been informed of Miranda's death, and, of course, I just got off the phone with her folks."

She got into the car and Bryers pulled out of the parking lot. As they took a left and headed for Highway 259 toward West Virginia, Bryers gave her a look she could not figure out. It was almost an amused sort of smirk.

"What?" she asked.

"You're a natural at this, you know?"

"No I'm not."

"Yes, you are. You had those men calm within thirty seconds. And you're able to dole out instructions without being condescending. They listened to you—and not just because you're pretty. What I just watched you do in the wake of that mess was nothing short of amazing. I have faith in you," he said.

It was a nice thing to say and Mackenzie appreciated the sentiment. But as images of Miranda Peters's head flashed through her mind, Mackenzie was not able to find that same sort of faith.

***

It was 3:17 when they arrived at the Peters residence. It was a simple little two-story house tucked away in a middle-class subdivision on the outskirts of Moorefield. When they stepped out of the car and started for the house, Mackenzie could already hear the wails of the grief-stricken mother before they even reached the front door. She and Bryers exchanged an uneasy look as Mackenzie raised her hand and knocked on the door.

The door was opened and a short overweight man greeted them. Behind a pair of thick glasses, his eyes were red and filled with a pain that seemed to leap out at Mackenzie.

"You're the agents?" he asked. His voice was hoarse and thick. It was very clear that he had been crying profusely.

"We are," Mackenzie said. "If you think you can manage, we need to ask some questions."

"I'll do my best," he said, extending his hand. "James Peters. And I have to apologize, but I don't think my wife will be participating. She's locked herself in Miranda's bedroom and I don't—"

James Peters let out a huge sob and nearly fell into the floor. Bryers stepped in to support him and when he did, the small man leaned into Bryers and wept openly. Bryers did his best to comfort him as he led him back into his house. Mackenzie stepped inside and closed the door behind her. From elsewhere within the house, she still heard Mrs. Peters wailing.

"Mr. Peters," Mackenzie said as the three of them stood in the small foyer. "We can come back later if you need us to."

"No, it's fine," James Peters said through tears. He choked back a sob and finally removed himself from Bryers. "Come on in. Officer Smith said it was a time-sensitive matter."

"Well, yes," Mackenzie said. "If you can provide any details at all that could help us, it would be appreciated. We believe that all of this happened within the last twelve hours or so. Being so recent, the more information we have, the less time the man that did this has to get away."

"So what do you need to know?" James asked. There was still extreme sorrow in his face but there was also determination. Anger lurked behind it all as well.

"Do you know if Miranda ever visited Little Hill State Park before last night?" Mackenzie asked.

"I have no idea. After she started college, she did the usual college thing. She kept to herself. She'd call us every now and then just to say hi. But as far as what she did with her spare time, I'm not sure."

"Had you ever met this girl she was supposed to be meeting with? Cho Liu?"

"No, but we had heard Miranda talk about her. They seemed to be developing a nice friendship."

A loud wail came from upstairs. A word was layered in this one, a word that sounded like a guttural cry of *"Miranda!"*

James looked upstairs, his heart breaking. He then looked to Mackenzie and Bryers. The torment in his face made Mackenzie feel almost physically sick. She felt beyond sorry for this man but was grateful that he had not seen the state his daughter had been in.

"I know...this is terrible," Mackenzie said. "We'll leave you to your grieving as quickly as possible."

"Yes, please...I—"

And then he started crying again. He couldn't look at them but gave them a go-ahead gesture as he wept.

"Can you think of anyone that might have had something against Miranda? Is there anyone that she had trouble with in the past?"

James's head suddenly shot up and looked directly at them. An estranged sort of realization floated in his eyes for a moment, snapping the flood of sobbing shut for a moment.

"Rick Dentry," he said.

"Who is that?" Bryers asked.

"An older guy that Miranda saw behind our backs when she started high school. He had just moved into town and had this weird obsession with her. He had already graduated from some other high school when they started seeing each other."

"So they dated?" Mackenzie asked.

"For a while, I guess." He spoke clearly now, the anger and possible connection dawning on him more and more. "But when we found out, Miranda called it off. Only Rick kept coming around. One night while Tabby—my wife—and I were out on a dinner date, he came to the house. Miranda went outside to speak with him because she knew she'd get in trouble if she let him in the house. He...tried to rape her."

Tears came out of his eyes, fresh and free flowing. These, Mackenzie thought, were the direct result of furious anger.

76

"Were the police involved?" Mackenzie asked.

"Yes. We filed a restraining order against him. It got pretty ugly because he'd ride by here and sort of scope the house out."

"When was the last time you saw him?" Bryers asked.

"Miranda's junior year of high school."

"You said he moved here from somewhere else," Mackenzie said. "Do you know where?"

"I'm not positive," he said. "Not too far away. Miranda never really talked about him in depth."

Mackenzie shot Bryers a glance and he nodded. He grabbed his cell phone and stepped out of the room, back into the foyer. As he left, she heard him coughing again. She'd caught him doing it several times today, but not nearly as bad as it had been yesterday.

"Agent White," James said. "Can...can we see her? It doesn't seem real."

"Not just yet," Mackenzie said, cringing at the thought of someone having to explain to the Peterses just how badly their daughter had been hurt. "The scene is still being combed. But someone will be in touch with you shortly."

Again, James lost himself to his sorrow. He collapsed onto the couch and bawled into a cushion. He was easily fifty-five years old but he looked like a little boy in that moment. Mackenzie could do nothing more than sit there awkwardly and wait for it to pass.

After a few moments, Bryers stepped quickly back into the room. "A quick background check on Rick Dentry, formerly of Moorefield, West Virginia, reveals a very interesting list of residences before *and* after moving to Moorefield."

"Like what?" Mackenzie asked.

"Like a brief stint in Strasburg, Virginia, while in grade school. He then moved with his family to Moorefield. He stayed here until three years ago when he worked in Roanoke as a furniture delivery guy. But then he moved back to Strasburg, where he currently lives."

"Holy shit," Mackenzie said.

"Oh, it gets better. He's currently working as a saw operator with a logging company in Strasburg. He's been doing that for eight months now. But would you like to know what he was doing before that?"

"What?"

"He was training as a river tour guide for Little Hill State Park."

CHAPTER FIFTEEN

Apparently, Rick Dentry had just gotten off of work. He was standing by his pickup truck, taking a chainsaw and a can of gasoline out of the back, when Mackenzie and Bryers pulled into his dusty driveway. Rick Dentry eyed them suspiciously and stood at the back of the truck as they got out. He had long hair that touched his shoulder and a beard that was in need of a trim. Behind him, Dentry's single-wide trailer looked like a strong wind might blow it over without much trouble.

"Can I help you?" Dentry asked as Mackenzie and Bryers stepped out of the car. He had a thick country accent that made the four words sound like two, spoken in some bizarre foreign language.

Mackenzie flashed her badge and took a few steps toward the truck. "I'm Agent White and this is Agent Bryers," she said. "We're working on a case where your name came up and we were hoping you'd cooperate by answering some questions."

"A case where *my* name came up?" he asked.

"Yes," Mackenzie said. "About five years ago, you were involved with Miranda Peters, correct?"

He looked a little shocked. She watched as he processed the question and waited for him to trip himself up. On the way to Dentry's house, Clements had called with a few facts about Dentry's past. There was the restraining order placed by the Peters as well as two speeding tickets. There had also been a domestic abuse complaint filed by an ex-girlfriend that had later been waived when it turned out that the ex-girlfriend had ended up in jail for petty theft and aggravated assault—not exactly the best of sources.

In other words, he had a fairly clean record. If he was their guy (and Mackenzie already doubted it), he'd have to slip up in order to incriminate himself.

"I don't know if you'd say *involved*," Rick said, finally answering the question. The look on his face made it clear that it was not a topic he cared to talk about.

"You were involved enough to have a restraining order placed against you," Mackenzie pressed.

"Oh, that." He laughed and rolled his eyes. "Yes…a girl a little younger than you enjoys having sex with you until Mommy and Daddy find out. And then you're suddenly a bad guy."

"You had sex with her before the night you attempted to rape her?"

He smirked. "That wasn't attempted rape. That was her being a little tease and then getting too worried about what her asshole parents would think about us."

"For your information," Bryers said, "her parents are currently—

"Look," Rick interrupted in a shout. "I've stayed the hell away from that family ever since the restraining order was put down. Ain't no woman worth that amount of trouble. So if this is what that's about—"

"It's not," Mackenzie said. "At least, we hope not."

"Then why the hell are you here?"

"Because Miranda Peters was found dead this morning," Mackenzie said. "She'd been murdered in one of the most graphic ways I've ever had the displeasure of seeing."

She studied Rick's face as she revealed the information. Most of the time, she could read a reaction well. She knew genuine surprise and shock when she saw it. Something indeed came across Rick's face but she wasn't sure it was shock or disbelief. It looked more like sadness. Regret, maybe.

"You think I did it?" Rick asked. "Is that it?"

He sounded furious and she could also hear some sadness in his voice. Seeing the look on his face and hearing the hatred in his voice, Mackenzie became very aware of the fact that Rick was still holding the chainsaw in his hands. She was also aware that he was more worried about being accused of the crime than about Miranda's death.

"No, we're not accusing yet," Mackenzie said. "Right now, it would be extremely helpful if you could simply prove your whereabouts last night."

"I could do that easy enough," he said. "But it's none of your damned business."

"Oh, but it is," Mackenzie said. "See...I have *almost* enough reason to slap cuffs on you right now."

"Bullshit."

"Tell me, Mr. Dentry...why did things not work out for you being a river guide for Little Hill State Park?"

He looked to the ground and let out a stubborn chuckle. "That's none of your business, either."

"All I have to do is make a call to find out. But I've been riding around and making phone calls all day. Mr. Dentry...would it interest you to know that Miranda's body was found in the woods of Little Hill State Park?"

That comment seemed to disarm him. And this time, the expression on his face spelled it out for Mackenzie: this was definitely not their guy.

"What?" he asked. "How?"

"That's what we're trying to find out," Mackenzie said. "So please…help us eliminate you from the equation quickly."

"I got fired from the river guide thing because of my drinking problem," Rick said. His voice was still stunned and it made Mackenzie wonder if he had, deep down, harbored some very real feelings for Miranda Peters at one time. "My supervisor was Debbie Henderson. Give her a call if you want. She'll tell you."

"And how about last night?" Bryers asked. "Do you have a reliable alibi?"

"I came home, had dinner, and then went to the bar. The Oak Post, it's called. I can give you the names of at least five other guys that can confirm I was there until about eleven."

"And after that?" Mackenzie asked.

Rick hitched his free thumb over his shoulder. "After that, it was home sweet home. I have to wake up at five o'clock to get out to the job site."

"Mr. Dentry, when was the last time you saw Miranda Peters?" Mackenzie asked.

He thought about it for a while and frowned as the memory came to him. "She must have been a junior in high school, I guess. I got weak…I drove by her house a few times one day and hoped to see her, you know? On the fifth or sixth time by, I saw her. She was watering her mom's flowers out in the front yard. Looked real pretty."

"Is there anything else you'd like to add?" Mackenzie asked, now more certain than ever that Rick Dentry had nothing to do with Miranda's death.

"No," he said. "Just…God, she's *dead*?"

"Yes, I'm afraid so," Mackenzie said. "One more thing, Mr. Dentry. How well would you say you know the grounds around Little Hill State Park?"

"Decent, I guess. There are parts that are really just nothing more than woods and overgrowth, though. A lot of nothing."

"Do you know of anywhere people might be able to hide?"

"Not right offhand," he said. "But you know, there are stories about homeless people that used to camp out around the park. When I was trying the guide thing, I don't think it was a problem anymore, though."

"Thank you," Mackenzie said. "We appreciate your time."

She and Bryers got back into the car. As they backed out, Mackenzie saw that Rick Dentry was still standing by the back of his truck. He still held the chainsaw as if he had no idea what to do with it.

"You think he's clean?" Bryers asked.

"Yeah, he's not our guy."

She looked back to him one more time in the rearview before Bryers pulled them back out onto the road. Rick Dentry looked like a man deep in thought, perhaps looking back into his past for the single moment where everything had gone wrong for him.

CHAPTER SIXTEEN

It was 5:15 by the time they were done at Rick Dentry's house and Mackenzie was exhausted. The mere idea of driving back to Quantico only to turn around and make the trip again the next day made no sense to her. It made no sense to Bryers, either. While Mackenzie was driving, he called up McGrath and asked for authorization to stay overnight in Strasburg.

Twenty minutes later, they were checking in to a small yet surprisingly quaint motel. They got two single rooms and when Mackenzie stretched out on her bed upon closing the door behind her, she could hear Bryers in the room next to her. He was coughing again. They were dry and bellowing coughs that were starting to concern her. But if he was going to continue to brush it off, she didn't see the point in worrying herself with it.

She nearly walked next door to see if he wanted to head out to grab a bite to eat but decided against it. She was tired, she could tell that he was tired, and she needed some time alone to process the day's events. She leafed through the phonebook she found on the bedside table and ordered Chinese food.

While she waited for the delivery, she sorted out all of the information she had pertaining to the case. She laid out each document on the bed and stood over them. She looked down at the grisly pictures of the bodies, the background reports on the leads that had, so far, turned up as only dead ends. There had to be a link here somewhere—a link other than Little Hill State Park and the condition of the bodies.

Or maybe that was the only link she really needed and she wasn't able to decipher it yet.

What am I missing? she wondered. *Is the answer to everything I'm looking for staring me right in the face?*

She looked over the handwritten notes from yesterday morning and added Miranda Peters to it all. In terms of the victims themselves, there were no real links. What she did know was that she was still unable to shake the feeling that Will Albrecht's disappearance nineteen years ago was connected. If anything, she almost felt like that was the hinge piece to it all.

But why? What was she missing?

She looked over a list of the body parts that had been amputated, looking for a connection there. It could be physically motivated. Maybe spiritually, too. Fingers legs, heads…what was the relevance to those pieces, if any at all?

She looked down at the information for the next twenty minutes, stalking from one end of the bed to the other. She didn't stop until a knock at the door broke her concentration when her Chinese food arrived.

She ate her moo shu pork and fried wantons slowly, finding it a little unsettling that she was able to eat anything at all with the crime scene photos staring her in the face. She tried to figure out what could drive a man to be so violent. Surely he was aware of his need for violence and that what he was doing was wrong. And if that were the case, his violence was probably intentional—as was the fact that he seemed to be dumping the bodies in scattered locations around the park.

Was he laughing at them, playing some deranged game of cat-and-mouse? No matter how much she looked at the maps of the park, she could see no connection—not in the sites where the bodies had been dumped or in the site of Miranda Peters's campsite. So what was it all for? She had never been one to believe that men killed for no reason. Even if insanity was at the root of it, there was always some underlying cause. Sometimes it was minor, like the killer having a fascination with other killers…an interest that became a sick fantasy.

But there was nothing fantastical about these killings. If anything, the very nature of the dismemberments spoke of something much more basic, more primal.

He wanted attention. That much was obvious. It made her think that the killer was either an only child who had never gotten accolades and praise from his parents or a sibling of overachievers who had never really fit in. And since the bodies were both male and female, that ruled out any motive of sexism.

What else? What else can I figure out about him?

Based on the crime scene photos, there was really only one thing that was driven home: they were dealing with a sick individual.

The hell of it was that she *knew* they'd catch the bastard if he kept dumping his victims on the park grounds. With drones overhead and extra security along the entrances to the park, there was no way he could keep getting away with it. They'd get him eventually but the question was how many more he could kill before giving himself away.

With her dinner mostly gone and nightfall having nearly taken over outside the motel room window, her cell phone rang from the bedside table. She looked at it as if it were an annoying insect for a

83

moment but figured she should answer it. When she picked it up, she saw a familiar area code that nearly made her ignore it anyway.

Someone was calling from Nebraska.

Her first thought was that it was Zack, calling to drag out the misery of having ever been involved with him even further. But this wasn't Zack's number, unless he was calling from someone else's phone. With her interest piqued, she answered the call with a quick, "Hello?"

"Hey. Mackenzie?"

The male voice on the other end of the line was familiar but she couldn't make the connection right away.

"Yes, this is Mackenzie. Who is this?"

"Hey, hot shot. It's Porter."

The name stunned her for a moment and the emotion that washed over her surprised her. Walter Porter—her partner from Nebraska PD. He had been a partner who had cared very little for her until her last days in Nebraska. And now, nearly six months after seeing him for the last time (in a hospital bed, no less), it was like getting a call from a ghost.

"Porter," she said, her voice sounding far away. "My God! How are you?"

"Me? Not too bad. With six years left before retirement, they finally decided to give me a shot at detective. Your slot, I guess. Hard shoes to fill. And how about you, *Agent* White?"

"Things are going good," she said. "The academy was an experience, that's for sure. But I made it."

"I'm glad to hear it. I know it means nothing to you, but I'm proud of you."

"That actually means more than you can imagine," Mackenzie said.

A brief silence passed between them and it was then that Mackenzie wondered why Porter was calling her. He had never been the type of guy to make a call just to catch up. Just as she was about to ask about the nature of the call, he finally got around to the point.

"Listen," Porter said. "I had to ask a favor just to be the one to make this call. I thought it might be best if you had this talk with someone you knew and not some stiff guy from the Nebraska State PD."

"What's wrong, Porter?" she asked.

"There's nothing *wrong*," he said. "But a few days ago some hot shot private investigator uncovered something that relates to an old unsolved case. It meant squat to him, but he turned it over to the state PD and they looked it over."

"What case?" Mackenzie asked.

"Well, as of this morning, the Nebraska State Police are taking another look at your father's case. It hasn't officially been reopened yet, but if it is, it's looking like it might come over to the FBI before too long. And...well, you know how they work. Personal interest and all that."

My father's case? Had she heard him right? The very idea of it sent a chill racing through her. Images of her father's body raced through her mind and for a dizzying moment, she felt like she was in the bedroom where he had died.

"You there?" Porter asked. His voice sounded as if it were a million miles away.

"My father's case? You're sure?"

"Positive."

"I won't be assigned to it," Mackenzie said.

"That's why I'm calling. To give you a heads-up. Maybe you can sneak a peek before it becomes a federal thing."

"Do you know what this investigator found?"

"I have no idea. I actually don't even know much about this new case myself. I'm trying to find out but didn't want to waste too much time before letting you know."

"What was the investigator's name?" she asked.

"A guy by the name of Kirk Peterson. You want his contact info?"

"That would be great. Can you text it to me?"

"You bet. Look...take care out there, hot shot."

"You, too, old man."

"Ouch."

Porter hung up, leaving Mackenzie with a strange sort of nostalgia swirling in her mind. First, hearing from Porter, and then having him dredge up memories of her father.

My dad, she thought.

She'd always wondered what it might be like to solve his case one day—maybe on her own, in her spare time. Until this morning, the case had been dead for more than twenty years. So what in God's name could have come about to cause the Nebraska State PD to give it a second look after all this time?

Mackenzie sat down on the edge of the bed, the case of the Little Hill State Park killer momentarily forgotten. She wondered who she could call that might clue her in to things back in

Nebraska. She'd never made friends with the state PD back home and knew that it would be hell trying to get through all the red tape.

Her cell phone pinged as Porter texted the contact information for Kirk Peterson.

Looking at it, she knew what she had to do. And it was not going to be easy. More than that, it was probably going to be risky.

She sighed and pulled up a number that made her sweat by merely looking at it.

She then pressed CALL and could only hope and pray for the best.

CHAPTER SEVENTEEN

The first call went to McGrath. As she waited for him to pick up, she felt herself growing nervous and anxious. Her stomach felt like it was tying itself in knots as the phone started ringing in her ear.

McGrath answered on the fourth ring and sounded oddly pleasant. *Good,* she thought. *Maybe I've caught him in a good mood.*

"It's Mackenzie White," she said.

"White, what are you doing? How are things there in Strasburg?"

"Coming along slowly, sir. But as much as I hate to say it, that's not why I'm calling. There's been…well, there's some things going on in Nebraska with my family. A pretty touchy severe family-related incident."

"Why are you telling me this?"

"I'd like your approval to go out there," she said. "It shouldn't take long. Maybe two days, if that."

McGrath was quiet for a while. When he answered, his good mood seemed to have died down a bit. "Do you think we need another agent out there to cover for you?"

"No, sir," she said. "As a matter of fact, we would likely have come back to the DC area tomorrow. I'll obviously stay as updated as I can through e-mails and phone calls while I'm away."

"That's fine," he said. "I'll sign off on it. I trust that Bryers can handle things in your absence. But at the risk of seeming heartless, I can't give you any more than forty-eight hours. Understood?"

"Yes, sir. Thank you."

With the call over, Mackenzie took a deep breath. She supposed she had just lied to him by omission. Of course, she knew if McGrath found out that she was going home to tackle a potential federal case before it actually fell under federal jurisdiction, he'd go berserk…and with good reason.

She knew she was risking a lot. McGrath was finally starting to warm up to her and she was involved in a fairly high-level case right now. To abandon it for reasons that could eventually cause her even more trouble and hostility with McGrath and his superiors was borderline foolish.

But this was her family. This was her *father*. And if she could finally solve his case and put it all behind her, maybe the terrible nightmares would finally stop.

Or, some wiser part of her thought, *revisiting it all could make the nightmares even worse.*

She thought of the dream she'd had about the rabbit—a skewed dream representing an actual event from her life. While it had been a variation that had taken her dreams out of the blood-soaked bedroom, it had still been terrifying.

But she had not thought of her father in that way in a long time. In that dream, if only for a moment, she had gotten to remember him as the kind and fun man he had been. It was a memory that the nightmare of the bedroom and her discovery of his body had robbed from her.

Choosing not to give that line of thought any footing, she gathered up all of the case notes on the Little Hill killer and tossed them into her bag without much organization—something that was very much unlike her. As she did that, she pulled up Expedia on her phone and booked the first flight she could to Lincoln, Nebraska. The best she could do was a flight out of Dulles at 11:05 p.m. with two stops before it would put her in Lincoln at 8:35 the following morning.

To get to Dulles, though, she'd have to have a ride. She toyed with the idea of calling a cab but that didn't feel right. In a moment of vulnerability that she had not expected, she knew that she wanted Bryers in on this. She did not want his help per se, but she needed to share it with *someone.* She felt safe in knowing that he would not rat her out to McGrath and, more than that, she was starting to really trust him as a friend and confidant.

It was just after eight o'clock when she knocked on his door. She had one change of clothes on her, in the trunk of the agency car—something she'd packed in the event they night need to stay over in Strasburg (which now seemed like brilliant preplanning on her part).

As he came to the door, she could hear Bryers coughing. It was almost a common sound now but it still made her worry.

He seemed surprised to see her at the door. He had also apparently gotten food delivered, as he was eating a huge slice of pizza.

"Hey, White. What's up?"

"So…I think I'm going to have to ask you if we can take a little drive tonight after all," she said.

"I thought the whole point of staying here was to avoid that."

"It was," she said. "But something…sort of came up."

He looked at her inquisitively for a moment and then frowned. "Are you okay?"

She felt like she might cry at any moment but managed to bite it back. "I don't know," she said. "But right now, I need you to take me to DC—to Dulles. If you can't, I'll get a cab. It's less than an hour and—"

"No, no, I'll take you," he said. "But…Dulles? What the hell for?"

"I just got a call from a man I worked with on the Nebraska PD. He was calling to give me a heads-up about a case…a case that looks to be linked to my father."

Bryers thought about this for a moment and nodded. "He called you to tip you off, didn't he? He wanted you to know before the feds picked it back up."

"Yes. And Bryers…I know it's asking a lot but I need you to keep it quiet. I sold McGrath on the idea of me going back but I wasn't totally honest with him. I just…I can't *not* check this out and—"

"It's okay," Bryers said. "We're talking about your father here. Your secret is safe with me. Just…be careful."

"I will. So, how about that ride?"

"Absolutely," he said. "Just let me get dressed."

***

Making the transition from the backwoods outside of Strasburg to the busy traffic trickling into Dulles was almost dreamlike for Mackenzie. She was distracted by the notion of her father's case being reopened. Even after she had told Bryers everything—from her father's death to getting the call from Porter—she found it hard to believe.

When Bryers pulled up to the curb at the airport, he popped the trunk and stepped out with her. Mackenzie grabbed her small bag and threw it over her shoulder.

"Thanks, Bryers," she said.

"Sure," he said. "Your secret is safe with me. But if you go past that forty-eight hours McGrath has given you, I'm afraid I can't help you."

"I know. I'm going to do my absolute best. And please keep me posted on any updates on the Little Hill case."

"I will," he said.

After a brief, awkward silence, Mackenzie turned and headed into the airport. She felt that her departure from Bryers had been too brief—almost rude in a way. But she was working against the clock here. She could deal with sentimentality later.

89

Inside the airport, she checked in, grabbed her tickets, and headed for the restroom. She locked herself in a stall, changed into the single change of clothes in the bag, and did her best to freshen up. At the sinks, she splashed some cold water into her face, tidied up her hair, and then went searching for her gate.

She sat down and realized that she still had an hour and a half before her plane departed. She wondered if she might be able to catch a nap in the uncomfortable seats but gave up on it after ten minutes.

As she waited, there was one thing that kept coming to her mind…something she knew she needed to do but didn't quite have the patience to endure. With a heavy sigh and an uneasiness in her stomach, Mackenzie took out her phone and scrolled to a name she had thought of often ever since moving to Quantico.

Stephanie.

To say that Mackenzie and her younger sister, Stephanie, had an estranged relationship was being far too gentle. They'd always been at odds; even before their father had died, when they had been scrambling through childhood, they had not gotten along. But it had been the years that followed their father's death and their mother's gradual descent into a psychotic break of sorts that had really hurt them. Stephanie had elected to let the grief and disorder of their life to define her while Mackenzie had worked extra hard to make sure she escaped it. This had eventually led Stephanie to a life of abusive relationships, meager jobs, and drama at every turn. Mackenzie, on the other hand, was currently in the midst of having achieved a goal she had set for herself after her father died.

With all of this history heavy on her heart, Mackenzie pressed CALL.

The phone rang four times before it was answered. Before she heard Stephanie's voice, there was a loud abrasive banging from the other end. Loud music pulsed through Mackenzie's phone from Stephanie's end.

"Hello?" Mackenzie said.

"Yeah?" Stephanie asked. "Who's this?"

"It's Mackenzie."

Again, she could only hear the blaring music in the background. Mackenzie assumed that Stephanie was out somewhere partying and drinking. She was pretty sure that's where about half of her sister's weekly paycheck went.

"Oh," Stephanie said, either simply confused or disappointed. "What's up?"

"I wanted to call to let you know that I'm going back to Nebraska for a while. I was wondering if you maybe wanted to meet for lunch or something."

"DC not doing it for you anymore?" Stephanie asked.

The tone of her voice and the edge of annoyance confirmed what Mackenzie had thought: Stephanie was out drinking.

"Well, I'm only going to be out that way for a day or so."

"Okay," Stephanie said, clearly not caring.

It's going to have to be this way, then, Mackenzie thought. "I'm coming back out there for Dad's case," she said. "Something came up in a state PD case that raised enough questions to have them take another look at the case."

Stephanie went silent again. The music continued to blare in her ear. It was some terrible current country-pop song. "Steph?"

"What the hell reason is there to open the case again?" Stephanie said.

"I'm not sure yet," Mackenzie said. "That's why I'm coming down there."

"And you're telling me *why*?" Stephanie asked.

"Because I thought you'd want to know. I thought you'd want—"

"No, Mackenzie. Fuck! Why can't you just leave this alone? He's dead. Nothing will change it. And whatever guilt has pushed you forever is wasting your time and energy."

"It's not guilt," Mackenzie said. Although, when the nightmares had been at their worst, she would often wake up with an emotion very much like guilt stabbing her in the heart.

"I don't care what it is," Stephanie said. "Look...thanks for thinking of me. But no. Leave me out of this."

Before Mackenzie could get out another word, Stephanie hung up.

Mackenzie slowly set her phone aside, wanting to scream, wanting to cry, wanting to punch a hole in the airport wall.

But she did none of those things. Instead, she found the closest coffee shop along the airport and sat silently as she waited for her plane to board as a dreary sort of anticipation swept through her. Her father's case was on the verge of being reopened.

And all of her worst nightmares were about to come to life.

CHAPTER EIGHTEEN

Brian Woerner had no idea what was going on in Little Hill State Park, but he intended to find out. He'd first seen the drone flying over the property when he had stepped out of his house to check his mail. He worked from home so anything out of the ordinary that happened outside was of great interest to him—even when someone did something as mundane as simple landscaping on his street.

He lived half a mile from the entrance to the park, so he had also noticed the police presence coming in and out of the park. That, added to the fact that he had seen the drone sweeping over the tree tops, made him think that there was something up.

Working from home as a blogger and non-fiction editor, Brian sometimes found himself researching interesting and often controversial things. Perhaps it was this facet of his work that gave him a particular bent toward a distrust of the government and favor toward conspiracies. And while there had been no unmarked black helicopters in the area, Brian found himself very interested in what might be attracting the police to Little Hill State Park. He was pretty sure the local PD didn't have the need or the budget for drone technology so *that* made him wonder of the feds were involved.

And that's what made him decide to do some research on his own. His blog usually centered on government conspiracies, from rigged presidential elections to grassroots UFO disclosure efforts. If there was something shady going on in Little Hill State Park, it would fit right in with his usual content. And he might even be the first to break the news.

Of course, a cursory drive into the park and by the visitor's center showed him that the park was closed down. There was no reason given, just a sign at the guard shack that stated that Little Hill State Park would be closed to the public until further notice.

The evidence of something fishy was just piling up more and more. And that's why he found himself taking a back road to the rear entrance of Little Hill State Park less than an hour after being turned away at the guard shack. As a twenty-five-year-old who had spent his teen years having lots of sex in the backs of cars and beds of trucks in these woods, he knew every nook and cranny of the park. He had, in fact, spent most of his free time as a fifteen- and sixteen-year-old purposefully walking the park in search of places to bring girls.

So when he saw a park ranger Jeep blocking the rear entrance to the park, Brian didn't despair. He knew of at least four other avenues into the park—at least two of which he was pretty sure the park rangers wouldn't bother blocking off.

He wound back through the back roads again, this time parking his car at the mouth of what had once been a dirt road used by hunters back when he'd been a small child. He locked up his car, took his phone and camera with him, and started walking.

Several feet up the old entrance to the dirt track, an old chain hung between two wooden poles. A simple No Trespassing sign sat in the middle of the chain, riddled with bullet holes. Brian ignored this sign (as he had done as a teenager) and walked a few yards further up the road before banking off into the forest. The thick woods were everywhere but he chose the thicker woods to the right.

He knew that right away, there would be a significant hill that would lead him down to flatter land. Because of his teenage wanderings, he had gotten to know these forests well. He never understood why people who claimed to love nature would stick to the paved walkways of a park when there was so much wilderness to be explored all around them.

At the bottom of the hill, a thin creek traced its way through the woods. He took a large step over it and when he was on the other side, he saw the line of wooden markers topped with red paint. The markers were about two feet high and, he knew, served as the physical border of where the Little Hill State Park eastern edge began. About a mile further through the forest, he knew he'd come to a dirt trail—a secondary footpath that would eventually come alongside the creek he had just crossed. It was much more scenic that the official trails in Little Hill but was also more of an adventure.

He was headed for that trail, pretty certain that he could use it to get close enough to the central paved trails. From there, maybe he'd be able to get a good read on what was going on. He walked quietly and kept looking to the sky. If the drone came by and he was spotted, he wasn't sure how much trouble he'd be in for managing to get around the park's public closing as well as the thin security set up at the secondary entrances.

It was during one of his sky checks that he heard the footsteps coming from out of the woods to his left.

Damn, Brian thought. *Did they have officers out here canvassing the place?*

He started to back slowly away, ready to run back the way he had come, hoping he could make it back up the hill without getting

93

winded. But just as he was about to start sprinting, he saw a man emerge from the thickness of the forest to his left. He was certainly not a cop and likely not a ranger, either. He was dressed in a black T-shirt and a pair of faded jeans. He looked like he might be confused—perhaps lost or turned around in the woods.

He was carrying something in his hands, hiding it behind his back. Brian couldn't tell what it was but he was pretty sure it was long. A rifle, maybe?

"Hey there," Brian said. "You sort of gave me a scare."

"Yeah?" the man asked. "Sorry. I didn't mean to."

The man came closer and closer, walking slowly. The closer he got, the more Brian could see that the expression on his face wasn't one of confusion. He wasn't sure what it was, exactly. The man's eyes were wide and he wore a thin smile on his face.

Instinctively, Brian took a step away.

"What brings you out to the woods on a day like this?" the man asked.

"Just sort of walking around, you know?" Brian said. "I was going to go the park but the cops seem to have that shut down."

Brian hoped the mention of the cops might startle the man. Still, the man came closer. It was then that Brian finally got a glimpse of what he was holding behind his back. It was an old battered axe.

"Yeah, the cops like to fuck around in places they aren't wanted," the man said. He looked around at the forest and then finally brought the axe out from behind him. "What good would they do in a beautiful place like this?"

Maybe it was the man's tone...or maybe the look on his face. Whatever it was, Brian did not like it. He started ambling backward without turning away from the man. Turning his back to this man suddenly seemed like a very bad idea.

Brian chuckled nervously in response to the man's comment about cops, mainly because he had no idea what else to do.

"You seem to have found a way into the park, though," the man said. "That's pretty resourceful."

"Well, I know these woods very well," Brian said.

"Yeah, I do too," the man said. "I know them very well."

Slowly, he reached into his pocket and withdrew his phone. He had the feeling that calling 911 very soon might be a good idea.

But just as he thumbed the lock screen on, the man came forward in a mad dash. He moved so suddenly and so fast that Brian barely had time to react. He let out a little yell of surprise and then turned around to run.

He made it three steps before the man caught up to him.

Something hard struck him from behind, colliding squarely with the back of his head.

Before the world went black and his head seemed to explode, Brian had just enough time to think: *He didn't get me with the sharp end of the axe, but the flat end. I'm not dead.*

I'm not dead yet.

CHAPTER NINETEEN

Mackenzie had managed to fall asleep on the final stretch of flight to Lincoln after ping-ponging sleepily through the stops and brief layovers in between. She awoke to the sound of the captain announcing that they would be landing in ten minutes and when the wheels hit the ground, it would be 8:07 Nebraska time.

She wasted very little time, only stopping at a little pastry shop within the airport to grab a muffin and a coffee before heading to the rental car desk. It wasn't until she was behind the wheel of her rental that she realized she had never even bothered coming up with any sort of plan. It had been intentional, though. As much as she hated to admit it to herself, she hadn't wanted to go into this with any sort of plan. She didn't want to overthink it—especially when she now had less than forty hours to be back in Strasburg.

Before pulling out of the rental car lot, Mackenzie opened up the text Porter had sent her. She didn't hesitate at all as she tapped on Kirk Peterson's number. He answered on the first ring, as if he had been waiting for her call all morning.

"Hello?" he said.

"Kirk Peterson?"

"Speaking," he said.

"This is Mackenzie White. I'm with the—"

"I know who you are," he said with a hint of slyness in his voice. "Your friend Walt Porter told me you'd probably be calling."

"Well, I was hoping you'd have the time to meet with me."

"You're in Nebraska?" he asked, surprised.

"Yes. Lincoln."

"In that case, yes, I'd be happy to meet with you. Do you drink coffee?"

She looked to her cup she'd gotten in the airport, sitting mostly empty in the cup holder of the console. "Yes."

"Let's meet for coffee, then," he said. "I can meet you in half an hour."

***

Mackenzie's first reaction to meeting Kirk Peterson was that the man was gorgeous. When he smiled at her as she sat down across the table from him at a Starbucks ten minutes away from the airport, she thought he looked like a more masculine version of Ryan Reynolds. He was ridiculously handsome but had a gruff

96

quality to him that made her think he would be a great wilderness explorer. He looked to be in his mid-thirties. A five o'clock shadow painted the lower half of his face and a set of deep brown eyes dominated the upper half.

He was dressed in a basic white button-up shirt, a tie, and a pair of dark jeans. Aside from his cup of coffee, he also had a single file folder sitting on the table.

"Hey there," he said, offering his hand. "Kirk Peterson."

"Mackenzie White," she said. "Thanks for meeting with me."

"Of course. I understand that this recent case might have potential links to the death of your father."

"Well, that's what Porter says," she said. "But he didn't have much information."

"Be straight with me here," Peterson said. "You're trying to get a jump on this before it lands in federal hands, right?"

"Right."

"In that case, I think you should hear about the case I just wrapped up." He slid the folder over to her but did not take his hand off of it right away. "You might want to lean over it. If someone walks by and sees some of the pictures in there, they might upchuck their chai teas and mocha lattes."

She opened up the folder, leaning in. As she started looking through the documents and photos, Kirk Peterson started giving her the basics of the case.

"It started off as a wife calling me up to bust her husband for potentially cheating on her *and* slowly wiping out their son's college savings. So I staked him out and found out that he was not cheating on his wife but he *was* having some late-night meetings with a group of people I am fairly certain are part of a drug cartel operating out of New Mexico. This made no sense because this guy was clean as a whistle. No record, no priors, assistant coach on his son's Pee Wee football team, the whole ten yards.

"So once I got enough proof to present the wife and the police, I knew that I had to make a hard call—a call that would shatter a perfect suburban life. Only, about half an hour before I made the call to the wife, I got a call of my own. It was from the local PD out in Morrill County, where the guy lived. His wife found him dead in their bedroom from two bullet holes to the back of the head. She was in the house when it happened and does not recall hearing any gunshots."

Mackenzie looked to the several photos in the folder. Her heart skipped a beat. The pictures could have been ripped straight out of her nightmares. A man lay face down on his bed, blood on the sheets, headboard, and walls. She could not see the man's face, making it that much easier for her to imagine that it was her father.

"And you're certain the wife didn't do it?" Mackenzie asked. "She thought he might be cheating on her. Maybe she got jealous and—"

She trailed off, already feeling that it was a thin thread to chase.

"I thought the same thing," Peterson said. "But it doesn't check out. The police are certainly looking into it and I'm sure the feds will grill her hard when they take it over. But I can almost guarantee you that the wife didn't do it."

He paused here, as if waiting for her to catch up. She still had a few documents to go through, mostly crime scene photos that, thankfully, did not include the body. She thumbed through the rest almost casually but then stopped when she neared the end.

She blinked her eyes impulsively to make sure they were working right. She stared down at one of the pictures…a document where two images had been placed side by side. For a moment, she literally forgot to breathe.

"Yeah," Peterson said. "I wanted you to see that for yourself. There's no way I could have explained it properly."

She only nodded. The document showed two images. One was the front of a business card and the other was the back of the business card with something scribbled on it.

"This was found on the scene?" she asked.

"Yeah."

She stared at it even longer. The front of the business card read:

Barker Antiques: Old or New Rare Collectibles.

The words stung her heart. She'd seen this business card before—but not this *exact* business card.

It had been found in her father's pocket after his death.

But the words on the back of this one made it quite unique. There had been nothing on the back of the card found in her father's pocket nearly twenty years ago.

She looked to the words and felt a weak little cry crawling up her throat.

There was a name scribbled on the back of this new card, written in thin, leaning cursive.

Benjamin White.

Her father's name.

CHAPTER TWENTY

"This makes no sense."

The words felt thin coming out of Mackenzie's mouth. Twenty minutes had passed since she'd seen the picture of the business card and they had promptly left the Starbucks. They were currently in Peterson's car. He was driving as she looked numbly through the documents again.

"I know," Peterson said. "Maybe visiting the scene will help. I understand that you have a knack for dissecting a scene."

"You said this was in Morrill County?"

"Yeah. The house is about an hour and forty minutes away. You okay to be in the car with me for that long?"

An hour and forty minutes, she thought with some dry humor. *Just shy of the distance between Quantico and Strasburg.*

"Yeah," she said. She was no longer sidetracked by his looks. The light weight of the folder in her lap felt heavy now, the only thing her brain could focus on. She looked to the photos of the man on the bed—a man named Jimmy Scotts, according to the information in the file. She did her very best to not impose her father's image over the pictures but it was hard.

"That connection," Peterson said. "The business card. You have any ideas?"

"None," Mackenzie said. "When my father was killed, the cops and the FBI searched everywhere but could not find a Barker Antiques. There was one place in Maine, but the business card was very different and was owned by a seventy-year-old veteran. They checked the place out tirelessly but there was no connection."

"I got the same results," Peterson said. "The place seems to not exist."

"But why would someone print up business cards for a fake business?"

"Beats me," Peterson said. "It's like you said…it makes no sense."

That's an understatement, she thought as she finally looked away from the folder to her lap and to the eerily familiar Nebraska landscape out of Peterson's window.

***

Their circuit through Morrill County took them on a route that featured Chimney Rock out in the distance. Mackenzie watched it crest in the distance and, for the first time, realized that there was something about Nebraska that she missed. The beauty of the long stretches of land, the isolated feel, the wide open skies.

Her nostalgia was short-lived, though. Twenty minutes after putting Chimney Rock in the rearview, Peterson pulled his car into a small suburban neighborhood. He took a few turns deeper into the neighborhood and finally came to a stop in front of a cute two-story home.

"The wife is with her sister right now, out in Omaha," Peterson said. "She already gave me the go-ahead to revisit. The local police are okay with it, too. Honestly, I think they're sort of hoping the feds sweep in here as quick as they can."

They stepped out of Peterson's car and entered the Scotts residence. While the place was empty, it had the feel of a space that had recently been filled with people coming and going; it was a feeling Mackenzie had grown accustomed to ever since starting her position as a detective not too far from here, actually.

Peterson led her through the house, toward the bedroom. She took note of the box of tissues on the coffee table in the living room. Several crumpled used ones littered the table and the floor. She observed every detail she could find just to distract herself: a slightly crooked picture frame on the wall, the dust on top of a decorative lamp stand in the hallway, and a Superman figure lying in the floor outside of a bedroom further down the hallway.

But she could no longer distract herself when Peterson opened the last door along the hallway. He pushed it open and Mackenzie followed him inside.

The bed had been stripped but the scene otherwise looked just as it did in Peterson's photos, sans a body. The splatters of blood on the wall and headboard remained.

"How long ago was he killed?" she asked.

"About forty-eight hours or so," Peterson said.

"And has anyone been in here since you left that you know of?"

"I don't think so. Maybe some forensics guys from State. Just because this was originally my case, I'm not exactly a cop, no matter how much the wife tried to place me in charge of it."

Mackenzie walked slowly around the bed. She grimaced when she studied the blood splatters on the wall. They went at a slight right slant, indicating that Jimmy Scotts had been shot at something of an angle; the shooter had likely been standing just to his left when they pulled the trigger. Scotts had also probably been asleep to have been shot in the back of the head and not stirring at all.

"You said the wife was home when it happened?" she asked.

"Yeah. In the living room, watching Jimmy Fallon. She didn't know he was dead until she came to bed and felt the blood on the sheets."

"If Fallon was on, this was probably between ten thirty and eleven thirty, yeah?"

"That's what we figure."

"And you're sure the wife wouldn't be a suspect?"

"Extremely doubtful."

"Any chance I could talk to her?"

"I can give you her information if you *really* want it, but she won't talk to you. She's devastated. And I doubt you could talk to her later. Not unless you can work some magic to get yourself assigned to the case."

She studied the room, looking behind her. There were two windows along the rear wall. She walked to them and checked them for signs of breaking and entering. There were a few scuff marks along the outer rim of the frame, but nothing damning.

"I'm heading out back," she said.

"Going to check the windows?" Peterson asked. "I did that. But just to cover my bases. What are you thinking?"

"I'm thinking the blood splatter is at an angle and that the shooter *had* to be behind him and shooting from the left. I also think he was very quiet but not quiet enough to come through the window right beside the bed. One of these windows has to be where the guy came in from. That or the front door."

Peterson made a *hmmm* sound as he followed her out through the front door and around the side of the Scotts' yard. The backyard was tiny, the lot overtaken by a thin strip of trees that separated most of the block from the next block over. The yard itself was maybe a quarter of an acre, not very large at all.

She went to the window and found it just slightly too high to look into. This instantly made her look to the ground. She looked for any signs of clear indentations—of the shooter having to use something as a stepping stool of sorts to get to the window. She searched for two minutes and came up with nothing. She then scouted the yard for any object someone could use to climb a bit higher to the window. Again, she saw nothing. There was a red bike, presumably Jimmy Scotts' son's, leaning against the far back wall of the house, but a quick check of it showed no signs of someone having used it as a makeshift stepladder.

"Need a boost?" Peterson asked with a smile as she started looking to the windows again.

"No thanks," she said, trying not to sound cold.

They went back inside, back to the bedroom. There, Mackenzie opened the windows, popped the screen out, and peered into the yard. With her head sticking out of the window, she could get a pretty good look at the outside frame. Again, she could see nothing to indicate forced entry.

She looked back to the stripped bed. "Has anyone checked the victim's contacts to see if he knew anyone that might know of a place called Barker Antiques?"

"Not that I know of. You think someone should?" he asked.

"Yes. And the bureau will assign someone to it when they take over."

With that, she started for the hallway. Peterson fell in behind her, clearly a little intimidated by her. "You done here?" he asked.

"Yes, I think so," she said. "You mind taking me back to...?"

"To where?" he asked. "Your car?"

She thought for a moment before asking: "Do you have anywhere to be anytime soon?"

"No. Not today."

"There's a little town about an hour east of here. Belton. You know it?"

"I do. That's where your father d—well, where you grew up, right?"

"How'd you know that?" she asked.

"I read the files on your father when this went down," he said. "It's sort of a part of my job as a PI."

"Well then, good work. You mind driving me? I figure it saves me a bit of time rather than having you drive me all the way back to Lincoln just so I can head back out."

"Not a problem," he said.

They went to his car and pulled back out onto the highway. They headed east and within several minutes, Mackenzie felt a tightening in her chest and an urgency in her breathing.

After twenty years, she was going back to the house where her father had died...the house from her nightmares.

She was, she supposed, going back home.

CHAPTER TWENTY ONE

It was no real surprise for Mackenzie to find that the house she had been raised in up until the age of eleven was abandoned. From the looks of it, it had been abandoned for quite some time. She wondered if any other family had even bothered with the place after her family had moved out nearly twenty years ago.

As a matter of fact, most of the town of Belton looked to be in the same shape. It had never been a big town, boasting a population of just over two thousand when Mackenzie had been a girl. On their way through, they'd passed multiple businesses with boarded windows and For Rent/Lease signs. Only a few places remained in business: the corner store, a barber, and the local café, which she was quite surprised hadn't gone under; it had been only hanging by a thread when she had lived here.

Her childhood home seemed to summarize the fate of Belton, Nebraska. The roof was mostly stripped of its shingles. The front porch was still standing but looked on the brink of collapse. The windows were filthy, covered in a brown tinge brought on by age and neglect.

"Home sweet home, huh?" Peterson asked as they walked toward the porch.

Mackenzie could only manage a weak chuckle. She looked to the left and saw that the house her neighbors had lived in was the in the same state. An old faded realty sign had long ago fallen over in the overgrown yard. Beyond the neighboring house, there was only forest. Mackenzie looked beyond her childhood home and saw thin trees behind it and, much further back, the start of a dying cornfield that started the line of someone else's property.

When she stepped up onto the porch, her heart leaped in her chest. *Are you really doing this?*

Before she had time to focus on that question, she pushed against the front door. She was not at all surprised to find it locked. She saw no signs of Realtor presence and it was clear the place had gone to ruin. No one owned it. No one cared about it.

With a sick sort of pleasure, Mackenzie lifted her leg and delivered a hard kick to the door. Her aim was spot on, connecting just below the knob. The door flew backward, taking a chunk of the old rotted frame with it.

"Shit," Peterson said. "You sure about that?"

"If it becomes an issue, the owner can charge me," she said.

Peterson shrugged and gestured her inside. "Your show," he said.

Mackenzie took a deep breath, steadied herself, and then stepped inside.

Seeing the house in such a state of neglect gutted her. There was no furniture, no pictures, and no real sense of living space. She just saw empty rooms, the carpet musty and discolored in most of them. This house had really only existed in her memories and those memories now felt like lies. This did not feel like the place she had grown up in, but rather some weird model of it.

Still, she knew which room had been the living room. She could also tell which room along the small hallway had been hers and which had been Stephanie's. She knew it all too well, like information that had been burned into her brain through the power of nightmares. She knew full well that she could spend time in each of those rooms and come up with a few memories—some that might even do her some good.

But she wasn't here to reminisce. She was here to face her past, to face a moment that still haunted her—to face a moment from her childhood that had all of a sudden come back into her life in a very real and unexpected way.

She skipped all of the other rooms and headed directly toward the back of the house. She could see the door to her parents' room and for a terrifying moment, she was certain it was no different from the night she had pushed it open and discovered her father's body.

She felt her hands trembling. Her heart was like some motorized piston in her chest. She stopped in front of the door, frozen for a moment. Then, without bothering to turn toward Peterson, she said: "I'd like some time to myself if you don't mind."

"Of course," Peterson said. "I'll be out at the car. Just yell if you need me."

She nodded absently, still staring at the door.

When she heard Peterson walking through the front door, his footfalls creaking on the old porch, she reached out to the door. With a hand that felt weightless, she pushed it open.

For a moment, she felt like she was falling.

What are you doing? What the hell are you doing here?

The room looked much bigger without any furniture. Without the bed in the center, the anchor to all of her nightmares, it felt like a chasm.

Still, it was unmistakably her parents' old room. There was the small dent from the bedside table on her mother's side of the room, the tacky ceiling fan in the center of the ceiling, and, of course, the faint maroon splatters on the carpet that had never come up. She slowly walked into the room and stood under the ceiling fan, directly where the bed had once been. She breathed in deeply and managed to not choke on the smell of dust, mold, and neglect.

The business card for Barker Antiques had been found in her father's pocket, just as it had been found in Jimmy Scotts' pocket. As she stood in the room, she wondered who had given it to him, where he had picked it up. Where exactly on this carpet had the person stood?

With no idea that there were tears in her eyes, Mackenzie went to the floor on her knees. She looked to the old dried blood splatters on the floor.

Something seemed to stir inside of her, almost like a snake shifting under a rock. Whatever it was, it seemed to wrap around her heart and send its tendrils all throughout her body. Any hint of sadness she had at revisiting this house was stamped out, replaced by what she slowly realized was a creeping sort of anger.

It made her feel nasty. It made her feel *dark.*

And maybe that was what she needed.

I hate this house, she thought. *Maybe I always did and just never understood it.*

She got to her feet and walked to the window that had, at one time, sat above her mother's bedside table. She looked out to the overgrown yard, the mostly dead tree standing just beside the driveway. This whole scene, just like this house, looked like something out of a muted black-and-white film.

It looked like something straight out of the past. And that's exactly where it belonged.

Out of nowhere, Mackenzie made a fist, drew it back, and punched the bedroom wall. Her fist went through the plaster and she was nearly ashamed that it felt so good. She pulled her hand out and found some of the skin peeled back. A tiny dot of blood sprang up in the plaster dust.

She took one last glance around the room and then walked toward the door. She didn't bother giving one last glance as she walked away.

The punch had been immature, sure. But now as she walked away from the room that had haunted her for so long, some part of her felt like she was finally leaving it behind her forever.

She slowly scanned the room, seeing the place through the eyes of someone who had, until about ten seconds ago feared it. Now it was nothing more than a ghost that had followed her, coming full circle back to where it had started to haunt her.

She tried to see the room through the eyes of a stealthy killer rather than the scared little girl who had found her father dead on the bed. It was a small room, made even smaller by the bed that had once been in it. According to the reports of the newest case, Jimmy Scotts' wife had been in the house when he had been killed.

Mackenzie reached way back into her past and recalled that everyone had been home the night her father had died. She and Stephanie had been in their separate rooms. Mackenzie had been getting ready for bed, reading a chapter in *Ramona the Pest.* Their mother had been asleep on the couch, passed out with a bottle of cheap wine at her feet and the TV playing soundlessly in front of her.

Mackenzie had heard the shot but hadn't realized what it had been. It wasn't until she thought she'd heard another sound that she got up to investigate.

What sound?

She stood there, frozen. Had she managed to somehow tuck this away, not wanting to think about it? Had revisiting this damned room unblocked it? Had it—

What sound, damn it?

Footsteps. She'd heard footsteps. And then the front door opening and closing quietly.

That's when she'd put her book down and gone out into the hallway. She'd gone straight to her parents' room, wanting to tell her dad that she thought someone was in the house...or someone *had* been in the house and then snuck out.

But the sight of what she had seen had locked that down and, she supposed, sent it spiraling into some subconscious hell.

Oh my God, she thought. *Someone came right into the house and did it. And Mom...she was on the couch asleep at the time...passed out and probably drunk and—*

Just like Jimmy Scotts' wife.

There was a connection there, a looming dark reality that she could not quite make sense of. There were far too many similarities to be a coincidence.

Does she know? Does Mom know? Did she—

"No," she said out loud.

But the thought finished itself in her head anyway: *Did she have something to do with it?*

CHAPTER TWENTY TWO

Peterson was waiting for her at the car, sitting on the hood and looking out to the dried up cornfield further out in the distance behind the house.

"You okay?" he asked.

"Yeah, I'm good," Mackenzie said. "Thanks for bringing me out here."

"Sure. Is there anywhere else you need to go?"

"No, I don't think so. I guess I need to get a flight lined up back to DC."

"Seems like a wasted trip," Peterson said. "Are you sure there's nowhere else I can take you?"

There *was* another place she had in mind, but she didn't see the point. It was a field from her past, the same field she had not been able to watch (but she had *heard)* her father put an injured rabbit out of its misery. Eerily enough, it had never been the rabbit that she kept thinking of, but the kite she had dropped.

Seeing that image in her mind nearly made her request that he take her there. It was a chunk of private property about fifteen minutes away—a place her family had used for picnics and countless games of catch.

But much like the bedroom she had just left behind, she knew that it was time to leave the field and all things associated with it.

"No, I'm good. Could you just take me back to my car? I think I'm just going to check into a hotel somewhere near the airport."

They drove in absolute silence for the better part of half an hour. She could tell that Peterson *wanted* to say something but was resisting the urge. Apparently, though, thirty minutes was his limit when it came to silence.

"So...this trip out here...was it like an exorcism of sorts?" he asked.

"What do you mean?"

"Well, you flew all the way out here to look at a recent crime scene and then a house that hasn't been occupied in at least fifteen years. You got nothing for your trouble and now you're heading back."

"Honestly, I didn't expect to find anything concrete," she admitted. "But what you showed me with the business card...it opens up a whole new level of things. And I don't have nearly enough time to properly investigate. I have to be back in DC tomorrow and it's already two thirty."

She kept the heart-wrenching revelation she'd stumbled across in the house to herself. It was, she thought, something she would hold close for as long as she could.

"You're okay with the feds stepping in and taking it over?" Peterson asked.

"I wouldn't say that I'm okay," she said. "But I guess I'll have to deal with it." What she didn't tell him was that she was already trying to think of some creative ways to ensure she stayed in the loop on the case once it landed in the lap of the FBI.

"I'll try to stay in the local loop down here as well," Peterson said.

"That would be nice. Thanks."

"So...how do you like the bureau as opposed to the detective beat down here?" Peterson asked.

"I like it. I think it's what I was always meant to do."

"It's not too stuffy?"

"It seemed like it at first...especially with going through the academy. But it's definitely been worth it. I mean...nothing is going to provide the freedom of being a private investigator, I suppose."

He smiled and looked at her with a mischievous wink. "It *is* sort of a glamorous life."

She was reminded of how good-looking he was when he looked at her like that. Where the hell had men like him been when she'd been wasting her time with Zack?

They went quiet again. Mackenzie looked to the scrape on her knuckles from where she had punched through the bedroom wall. She thought about how the house had deteriorated and felt freedom in it. The place that had haunted her nightmares for so long was not the daunting and horrifying place that was haunting her so badly. It was gone to ruin and looked sad. Maybe now that she had faced it, it would lose its power over her. Maybe now that she had unlocked the one secret it had been hiding from her, she could finally leave it in the past.

The ride back to the Starbucks where they had met six and a half hours ago seemed to be over far too quickly. Her thoughts had busied her, as had her weird almost unusual attraction to Kirk Peterson.

"You going to just sort of lay low for a while before going back?" Peterson asked.

"Yeah. I'll book a flight as early as I can in the morning. Seven or eight hours of solid sleep in an isolated room with nothing to do might be just what I need."

"Maybe a drink would help," Peterson suggested. "Maybe a drink with a certain private investigator?"

She considered it for a moment. What would be the harm?

The harm, she thought, *is that visiting your old house has taken you to a pretty dark place—and you don't need to layer that with alcohol and lust.*

"Thanks, but no," she said. "I truly do appreciate your help, but I think I just need to rest. This sort of...I don't know. The whole day took it out of me emotionally."

Peterson nodded, clearly disappointed but not saying as much. "I get it," he said. "But hey...I meant what I said. I'll keep an ear out down this way and reach out if anything develops. I'm sure your old friend Porter will do the same."

"Thanks, Peterson," she said.

She got out of the car and walked to her own, two spaces over. When she turned back, she saw that he was still looking at her. He was looking at her in the same way Harry sometimes looked at her—or, from time to time, the way Ellington looked at her.

Appreciating the attention, she got into her car and headed back toward the airport. She knew, though, that sleep would be a while off. Peterson had mentioned a drink and it was suddenly all she could think about. Perhaps just a few drinks in a hotel room by herself wouldn't be as potentially harmful as heading out to a bar with a gorgeous PI.

As she approached the airport, she kept her eyes open for hotels that didn't look like total dumps. If she was going to waste a night doing nothing more than getting better acquainted with her thoughts and theories on the Little Hill case (and, let's be honest, her father's as well), she could at least spring for a nicer room.

As she was scanning for a motel that didn't look like a roach trap, her cell phone rang. She read the name in the display and her shoulders sank. It was Bryers. And if Bryers was calling, there was probably bad news.

"Hey, Bryers," she said. "Miss me already, huh?"

"I do, actually. But that's neither here nor there," he said. "I hate to do this to you, but I need you to get back to Strasburg on the double."

"Why?" she asked, her heart thumping.

He cleared his throat and as a long pause followed, she knew it could not be good.

"Someone's gone missing in Little Hill State Park."

CHAPTER TWENTY THREE

Even after bumping her flight to a red-eye departing at 12:15 a.m. with a brief layover in Chicago, Mackenzie still didn't land in Dulles until after 9:10 the next morning. She beat out McGrath's forty-eight-hour allowance by almost a full eight but still felt late and as if she were holding up the case.

Bryers met her at the airport and filled her in quickly as he sped through the stream of traffic leading into DC. Bryers, however, was able to avoid the more clogged traffic as he got off on the interstate and once again headed back to Strasburg.

"Yesterday afternoon, one of the park rangers was patrolling the roads and happened to come across a parked car just off the road not too far from one of the maintenance roads at the northern end of the park. He followed a few slight disturbances in the foliage but could find nothing. There were some jumbled footprints but nothing we could use. Any other day, they wouldn't have thought twice about it. But given the circumstances, they looked into it pretty hard. We're expecting the State to have a helicopter out to the park for better aerial coverage by the end of the day."

"So who's the missing person?" she asked.

"They checked the plates on the car and found that they belong to Brian Woerner, twenty-five years old. A Strasburg resident. His house is actually a little less than half a mile away from the park."

"So he snuck into the park?"

"Seems that way. Only there was very little *sneaking*. He just knew the back roads and the old cutover roads. And that's *if* he went into the woods at all. But it certainly seems like he did. Clements and his guys checked Woerner's house and he wasn't there. We then checked with his family and no one has seen him for about two days. So right now, we're assuming he's the next victim."

"Shit. Bryers, I'm sorry I missed all of it."

"No big deal. We just don't have much time now, so you and I are headed straight over to his mother's house to get some information. She's already been told that her son is missing, so the hard part is over."

Mackenzie understood the sentiment behind such a comment, but she had no illusion of thinking the hard part was over. In fact, she couldn't help but feel that they had landed right in the middle of the hard part and now had to find their way out.

Wendy Woerner was understandably nothing more than a shell. It had been less than twenty hours since she had been informed that her son was missing and could very well be involved in a series of murders that had occurred in the area recently—murders she knew were attributed to what the media was labeling the Campground Killings.

When Mackenzie and Bryers took a seat in her living room, it was Brian's sister that responded the most to them. She was eighteen and, while it was clear the news had also taken its toll on her, she was doing her very best to stay strong for her mother.

The sister's name was Kayci and when she offered them coffee, Mackenzie accepted. She had not slept at all on the trip back to Dulles so she was only going on about six hours of sleep or so over the last two days.

"Does your brother make a habit of spending time out in those woods?" Mackenzie asked. She was very careful to use words like *does* rather than *did*. Using the past tense when the fate of her brother was not yet known could be very bad.

"Not that I know of," Kayci said. "As a matter of fact, he's not really the outdoorsy type."

"So it's safe to say that it was surprising to hear that he'd been out in the park?"

"Absolutely."

"When was the last time you spoke with him?" Mackenzie asked.

"Two days ago," she said. "He asked if I wanted to catch a movie with him. He doesn't have much of a social life so he relies on me as a friend most of the time."

"So he's something of a loner?"

"Yes, but by choice. He always shuts himself up in his house and stays online all the time. He has this blog that he basically lives for."

"What sort of blog?" Mackenzie asked.

Kayci rolled her eyes and smiled in remembrance of her brother. She pulled out her phone, typed in something really quickly, and then handed it to Mackenzie.

"That's his blog," she said. "He's a conspiracy nut. He got a Kickstarter campaign going to start a podcast but it never went through."

Mackenzie scrolled through some of the entries. There were articles Brian had written concerning the Illuminati, Bohemian

Grove, MK Ultra, and a recent attempt to infect the American population with a flu bug through local water sources.

A thought occurred to Mackenzie as she handed the phone back to Kayci. "Do you know if he keeps notebooks or files on stories he plans to write?"

"Tons of them," Kayci said. "He keeps them in moleskin notebooks. Mom actually has a few here; she went over there to do her own searching this morning and—well, it ended sort of badly. She brought a few of them back here."

"Could I see them?" Mackenzie asked.

"Sure. One moment."

Kayci got up and stepped into the adjoining room. When she left, Mackenzie took a moment to study Bryers. He looked dazed and very tired.

"You okay?" she asked.

He nodded but said nothing. He was not very convincing at all. She wondered if he was a little pissed that she had not been here when this part of the case had come to light. She wanted to press him a little more but by then, Kayci had come back into the room.

As she handed Mackenzie a pile of four notebooks, Bryers coughed behind her. There was a hollow sound to it, like a deep bronchial cough that had no phlegm to bring up.

As she flipped through the notebooks, Mackenzie hit pay dirt almost right away. The notebook on top of the pile was clearly his most recent, as the last entry inside of it was dated two days ago—the day she had left for Nebraska. There was only one note for that day, penned in an urgent and slightly sloppy print.

It read:

Heavy police presence at Little Hill State Park, complete with drones. Why? Missing persons, some weird state mandated research? Local news HAS said a body was discovered out there recently but doesn't give many details. What gives???

"Have you read this notebook yet?" Mackenzie asked.

"Yeah, I leafed through most of them," Kayci said. "But he was always like that...suspicious of the government. Why? Do you think the latest entry means something? I guess it would explain why he would have gone out there to the park."

"Maybe," Mackenzie said, although she was pretty certain it was a solid link. She drained the remainder of her coffee and got to her feet.

Bryers did the same behind her and Mackenzie took note that he was moving with great effort. He looked like he was on the verge of falling asleep. There was a look in his eyes that was almost glassy, making her wonder what the hell he had gotten himself into in the little bit of time she had stepped away.

Mackenzie extended her hand and shook with Kayci. "Thanks for your time and your help. We're going to do our very best to find your brother and make sure he gets home." She then turned to Wendy, still as motionless as stone in an armchair on the other side of the living room.

"Thanks again, Mrs. Woerner," Mackenzie said.

Wendy said nothing. She did not even nod. It was a morbid thought, but Mackenzie couldn't help but wonder if the mother had already resigned herself to the fact that there was a very good chance that when her son was discovered, he would be dead.

Mackenzie and Bryers left the house and headed for their car. "What did you think of that last note in his notebooks?" Mackenzie asked. "If Brian Woerner ran a blog dealing with mistrust of the government and conspiracies, he'd do just about anything to find out why there was a heavy police presence in the park—especially why there would be a drone. He seems like a real Alex Jones–type."

"That's got to be it," Bryers said, opening the driver's side door. "He spotted the drone flying over the park and got curious. Maybe he—"

He did not finish his sentence. In fact, as Mackenzie got into the passenger seat, she heard him make a soft coughing noise and then there was a thump along the side of the car. She looked over and saw that he had fallen over and was bracing himself against the side of the car.

Mackenzie rushed out of the car, running around the hood and going to his side as quickly as she could. She got there just in time; the moment she reached his side, he started to collapse, leaning to the left. Mackenzie caught him and he was nothing but dead weight.

"Bryers? Bryers, what is it?"

He shook his head and let out a heavy breath.

He took a moment to collect himself. Slowly, his strength seemed to return. He propped himself against the side of the car and blinked his eyes rapidly like a man who had suddenly been stirred away.

"Well, that's embarrassing," he said softly. "I'm sorry, Mac."

"Sorry? For what?"

"For not being honest. For not telling you sooner."

"Telling me what?"

113

He looked her in the eyes with the most emotion she'd ever seen from him and said: "I'm dying."

CHAPTER TWENTY FOUR

"Dying?" Mackenzie said, her voice panicked and a little too aggressive within the confines of the car.

Bryers had refused to speak about it right away. It had been ten minutes since his near-collapse. They were currently headed to the Strasburg PD to check in with Clements and Smith. Now that he seemed to have gathered his wits and had no fear of collapsing again, he seemed more open to talking about it. Still, Mackenzie had insisted on driving.

"Yeah. And pretty quickly, it would seem."

"How can you be so glib about it?" she asked. She was somewhere between angry and concerned and could not figure out which to focus on.

"I have to," he said. "The doctors are saying it's too late to really reverse anything. So it's either worry needlessly and say *woe is me* or I can go out on a better note."

"What is it?" she asked. "What were you diagnosed with?"

"Stage four pulmonary hypertension," Bryers said. "Apparently I've had it for years and just never knew it. By the time I saw a doctor for some slight chest pain and shortness of breath and they caught it, it was too late."

"My God," she said, the anger now fading out and letting concern take over. "There's *nothing* they can do?"

"There are treatments and experimental medicines with no real results. I could try them but they've told me the chances are slim. I could commit myself to staying in the hospital for all of those avenues but it could all fail and that would have me wasting the end of my life in a damned hospital bed. And I'm not doing that."

"How long do you have?" she asked.

Bryers shook his head. "I'm not having this conversation with you," he said. "The last thing I need is a partner watching over me like a child. No offense."

"And keeping this to yourself makes you seem like one of those old hermits that wants to be left alone. People that think no one can help them. *No offense*."

He smirked at her. "You know how to throw an argument, huh?"

"How long, Bryers?"

"On the high end, maybe eighteen months."

"And the low?"

He sighed and looked out of the window. "Maybe six."

"Jesus…"

"I'm fine with it," Bryers said. "Honestly, it's not affecting my day-to-day too much."

"Except for passing out randomly," Mackenzie said with some spite.

"Yes, except for that."

"How the hell is McGrath letting you work with such a diagnosis?" she asked.

"Because he doesn't know. I haven't told him. And you damn well better not, either. Remember, Mac…I'm keeping a secret for you, too."

She looked at him, aghast. "Bryers…you can't—"

"I'm not spending the end of my life in a hospital," he said. "But I will tell you this. I *promise* you this: when this Little Hill case is wrapped up, I'm done. I'll tell McGrath and go home to wait to die."

Mackenzie cringed. "Stop being so fatalist about it."

Bryers laughed out loud, a laugh that became a cough as it tapered off. "I'm dying, Mac. Seems like the *perfect* time to be fatalist."

Anger was creeping back in now—not just at the situation itself but her inability to control it. She thought she'd be the same way if ever faced with such information. She'd work and work up until the final moments when she could no longer operate. She set her jaw and did her best not to lash out at him—and her best not to start crying.

"I won't jeopardize this case," Bryers said "You have my word. If I start to feel faint again like I did in the Woerners' house, I'll let you know and I'll sit out for a bit."

"It's not the case I'm worried about," she said. "I'm worried about *you*."

"Like I said. It's too late now. So I'm just going to do my best to be useful with the time I have left. And please don't get offended when I say this, but I really don't want to talk about it anymore."

He said this last part in a stern voice that she had not heard from him in the past. It upset her, but again, she could see where he was coming from. She'd likely handle it the same way. So she said nothing. The car remained quiet all the way back to the Strasburg PD.

***

116

Three hours later, exhaustion hit her. Fortunately, it was after speaking with Clements and Smith, a meeting she had managed to get through without falling asleep. So far, there were no leads to the fourth victim other than his car, which had turned up no evidence. They had split up duties to keep the case going, with the park rangers canvassing the forest, Clements and his men working on a stricter barricade into and out of the park, and Mackenzie and Bryers tasked with digging deeper into who Brian Woerner was. Did he have enemies? Had he stirred up trouble on his blog?

Mackenzie figured she'd read through blog entries, particularly the comments sections, back in the hotel room until she fell asleep.

Those plans, however, were upended when they walked out of the Strasburg police station and she saw Harry Dougan standing by her car.

He smiled at her, as if he were bestowing some enormous favor upon her. She didn't even pretend to return it. She wondered why McGrath would send more agents out here when he knew damned good and well that with the park rangers, local PD, and the state PD, it was already something of a circus.

Bryers cut her a smile and got into the car. He gave Harry a half-hearted wave as he got into the passenger seat. He then scrolled through e-mails on his phone, giving Mackenzie a moment with Harry.

"What are you doing here?" Mackenzie asked him.

"I'm free for two days," Harry said. "I thought I might come up and see if I could lend a hand. I hear there's a possible fourth victim."

"We're good here, Harry," she said.

"You and Bryers? And the park rangers, I hear. Yeah…too many cooks in the kitchen, huh?"

"Exactly. Which is why I don't understand why you're here."

"I'm on my own time," he said. "I wanted to help. I wanted to see you."

"God, Harry, really? Look…I'm going to say this once with at least *some* sort of filter but after this, I can't promise niceties. I can't have you here right now. There's just too much going on and I can't add you to the pile of shit that's getting out of hand."

"Out of hand?" he asked. "What do you mean?"

She couldn't even look at him. For reasons she hadn't yet digested, the fact that he had showed up unannounced like some unwanted knight in shining armor pissed her off.

"What I mean is that there's a lot more going on in my life right now than just this case," she said. "And I don't need you here to make it more complicated."

"Well, I drove all this way. Can't we at least have dinner or something?"

"No, we can't," she said.

"What the hell is wrong?" he asked. "I thought you'd be happy to—"

"To *what?*" she yelled. "To politely dance around the fact that you have a thing for me that I have tried so hard *not* to flat out reject? It's not going to happen, Harry. And while you're a good agent, we don't need you here right now. So both of your reasons for coming up here uninvited are useless. So please…leave."

She saw the pain come into his face for only a split second before she turned her back to him and got into the car. She slammed the door, cranked the engine to life, and wasted no time backing out of the parking spot. She caught one more glance of him as she pulled out and felt a little heartless for not caring how hostile she had just been.

"Ouch," Bryers said.

She nodded, still pissed. "Yeah, I could have handled it better. But I don't have time to waste with…with trivial nonsense. I feel like we're running out of time."

Bryers nodded, looking gravely out of the window.

"I know the feeling."

CHAPTER TWENTY FIVE

The forests of Virginia at night were like some private orchestral performance as far as he was concerned. He listened to it while sitting in an old wooden chair and sipping from another Mason jar filled with what his father had once called White Lightning—a recipe that had been passed down through the men in his family ever since Prohibition had damn near ruined the country.

Honestly, he didn't care much for the taste. There wasn't much of a taste anyway. But he liked the burn. He liked the way it could make him feel almost disconnected from the world when he'd had enough.

He was usually filled to the brim with that burn when he set to work. Capturing the people to help him spread his joy was easy; they were brought to him, given to him by hands far gentler than his own. But when the time came to take the seeds from the people that he kept in the hole in the floor in his back room, he needed the burn. He needed to feel lighter than anything around him. He needed to be detached. It was gruesome work, but it was necessary.

He looked to the moon over the scraggly trees. He knew that just hours before, there had been something flying over the woods. One of those drones he'd read about in a magazine a few months ago. He guessed that meant the authorities were on to him. He'd known it would happen eventually. It was why he had paused for so long after the first victim. He'd gotten scared there, sure that the police would find out what he was doing.

But so what if they did? When he'd first heard the call, he knew that he would end up having to sacrifice himself. And that was fine with him. Who was he, but a servant to everything he saw before him? The trees shrouded in night, the scant clouds kissing the edges of the half-full moon, the songs of crickets, tree frogs, and even a loon or two off in the distance.

Yes, he had been called. He had been called to spill blood and return the living seeds of human flesh to the earth from which it had come.

He sensed that his work was almost done. Whether that meant that this fourth sacrifice would finish his work or that the police would soon find him, he did not know. And that was okay, because he was not *meant* to know.

With his head feeling heavy and his stomach rumbling, he went back inside his cabin. The smell of the moonshine he was making filled the place. It was fermenting in two large buckets in the back of his central living space. As he walked toward them, he could make out the sounds of his next sacrifice in the next room over.

He had learned a lesson with the last one. She had nearly escaped him, making him take another hard look at how he restrained the sacrifices. Being this close to the end, everything had to go perfect.

He wasn't ready to kill this one just yet. The sacrifices needed to suffer first. They needed to feel true danger, true hunger. They needed to appreciate their death when it was delivered. It made their flesh and blood more pliable for the soil—richer and more pure.

He walked into the addition to his small cabin. He looked to the benches, to the sledgehammer and the axe. He then looked to the plywood sheets on the ground, containing the next sacrifice. The man had fallen quiet about an hour ago and had not made a peep since.

Just to check, he stamped his foot down on the sheets of plywood. Instantly, the man hidden in the ground beneath them started to squeal. He was weeping, he was screaming, and he was begging all at the same time.

He nodded and walked back out to the buckets. The moonshine wasn't *quite* ready but it was close enough. He scooped some up in his jar, took a long pull from it, and felt the burn.

A day…maybe two.

That's when he would kill this man—the man that was likely to be the final sacrifice to the forest—to nature.

He wondered if he should explain his work to them before he killed them. Perhaps it would make them appreciate him a bit more. Maybe it would make the absolute certainty of death easier to accept.

But in the moment when he raised the axe or some other blade, he had seen something in their eyes several times: a blankness, an absolute shock of nothing, which seemed to carry them away right down to their final abrupt cry. And in that final moment, he knew there was no reasoning with them. They would understand nothing.

No one would ever understand—not unless they, too, had heard the call.

A call to set a corrected path for nature. A call to reset things, to thin things out.

He supposed he was doing God's work, really. He was removing the filth of human preoccupation into something divine. He was returning the blood, flesh, and offal back to the earth from which it had come. And in that, he was a saint.

From the back room, he heard the next sacrifice moaning weakly. The sacrifice seemed to already know that his time was short.

Some simply had to pay their debt sooner than others.

CHAPTER TWENTY SIX

Mackenzie felt defeated as she drove toward Quantico the following morning. She was eating a sausage biscuit she had grabbed at a drive-thru and wondering just how long she'd be able to keep up this pace. It was 6:45 when she and Bryers passed the Leaving Strasburg sign. They were leaving with no real leads and with a trail on the fourth victim that was unbearably cold.

She knew it was silly to feel defeated. But when McGrath had called and ordered them back because it seemed like a waste of manpower to stay near Little Hill, what else was she supposed to think?

The morning slogged on. When she finally got into her apartment just after eight a.m., she allowed herself a lingering shower. While standing under the hot water and letting her muscles loosen up, she did her best to prepare herself for a day filled with research and digging while knowing that a killer was very likely still active in Strasburg. The helicopter was set to start passing over later today and there was a fragile hope that it would help. She knew, though, that the State was stingy with resources and if there were no results within a day or so, the helicopter would be sent right back to wherever it had come from.

She left her apartment as quickly as she could, needing to feel productive. She went to headquarters and spent several hours compiling bios on the victims only to come to the conclusion that they had nothing in common. She even had an intern run cross checks to see if any of the user names in the comments sections of Brian Woerner's blog might be one of the other victims. But that turned out to be a dead end as well.

As if this wasn't frustrating enough, she had the other two monumental obstacles in her head: Bryers's announcement of his ill health and the eventual reopening of her father's case. She was expecting McGrath to call her at any moment to let her know that the bureau had taken on a new case in Nebraska that was linked to her father's old case but so far, there had been nothing.

And that, in a way, was good. Because she now had the sickening idea that maybe her mother had known about it. That would be a fairly big lead. And then questions would be asked about why she had not yet reached out and spoken with her mother.

And that was not something she was willing to answer just yet.

On the heels of all of that was knowing that she had totally mistreated Harry. Yet, while she knew it was a case of terrible timing on his part and nothing more, she was rather glad that it had come to that. The Band-Aid had been ripped off and she could now cleanly cut that questionable part of her new life away.

Shortly after she broke for lunch, still reading over Brian Woerner's blog entries for some sort of hope of a connection, she found herself looking at digital copies of the pictures that Kirk Peterson had provided. She stared at the business card for Barker Antiques, staring at both sides of it. Seeing her father's name written on the back was like looking at some relic from out of time, a new discovery that might help to reestablish previous views of a once-lost civilization.

This changed everything. This presented a whole new batch of questions surrounding her father's death. And the more she looked at it, the more she felt that not only was the man who killed Jimmy Scotts bragging in a subtle way, but he was also playing some sort of game…a game she didn't know the rules to. A game she didn't even know the name of yet.

She was mulling over this as she headed to the nearest coffee pot, which was located in a small alcove that served as a mini–break room of sorts. As she poured her fourth cup of the day, a familiar voice from behind startled her.

"Welcome back."

She turned and saw Ellington smiling at her. He looked bored and maybe a bit tired. He was also holding a cup of coffee.

"Thanks," she said.

"Were you starting to like Strasburg?" he asked. "I guess it beats the hustle and bustle around here."

"It's not too bad."

Ellington looked behind him, making sure the hallway was clear. He then stepped into the alcove and closed in on her. There was only about three feet between them.

"I'm going to ask you something. If you think I'm out of line, tell me to shut up. Okay?"

"I can do that," she said.

"I heard through the very long grapevine within the bureau that you took a trip out to Nebraska this week. Sort of an unexpected family thing. Is that right?"

She almost took him up on his instruction, telling him to shut up. But she was very interested in how he knew and why he cared.

"Yes, that's right," she said.

"Can I ask what for?"

"I'd rather you didn't," she said.

"Understandable. But I ask only because McGrath is currently seeking agents to assist with a case out that way. Somewhere out near Lincoln, I think. I read the brief on the case and there's a certain link to a certain old case that might interest you. Ringing any bells?"

"Are you going to bust me on this?" she asked.

"Absolutely not," he said, his voice quieter than ever. "I was just wondering if you managed to get a head start while you were down there."

"Off the record?"

He nodded, taking another peek down the hall to make sure they were still alone.

"The link to my father's case is undeniable," she said. "As of now, though, the only lead seems to be a false flag left by someone involved to send us scrambling. And no offense, but that's all I feel comfortable telling you."

"Got anyone down there that will be feeding you information?"

"Maybe. Why?"

"I can be a snoop on this end too, you know. It occurred to me when I read the brief that I really don't know all that much about your father's case. Seems a shame."

"Why is that?"

He cocked his head and looked at her inquisitively. "Because you interest me," he said. "Maybe a little too much."

A small flush of heat uncoiled in her stomach but she kept her head about her. "Those aren't words that should be spoken by a married man."

"You're right," he said. "But how about a man that got served with divorce papers two weeks ago?"

"Sorry to hear it," she said, meaning it.

"I was, too. At first. I'd love to tell you about it. Actually, that's a lie. I really just want an excuse to get out and have a drink with you."

"The need for a drink should be enough."

"I suppose so. So what do you say?"

"I say it sounds okay. But not now. There's way too much going on right now. I have to get this Little Hill case wrapped up. And this thing with the Nebraska case—"

He held his hands up in mock surrender and took a few steps back. "Say no more. I understand completely. The offer is there. Just call me when you want to cash it in."

With that, he walked away and he was gone. Mackenzie did not want to admit it to herself, but she wanted him to stay. The banter they were building felt normal. It felt safe and...well, like it was leading somewhere.

She went back to her cubicle and stared at the photograph of the business card again. She knew her mind should be on the Little Hill case. She felt like there was something she was missing...some huge clue that was sitting right in front of her, so obvious that it had been overlooked.

But still, the business card and her father's scrawled name were too hard to ignore. Someone had written his name very plainly, quite deliberately. But *who* had written it? For that matter, who would even know his name and how he had been killed?

My mother, for one, she thought.

Suddenly, she looked away from the files and folders. She slid the information from the Nebraska case aside and started quickly leafing through the photos and details of Little Hill. She looked to the locations within the park, noticing how they were all spread apart. She unrolled her map of the area and traced the points she had drawn on it with her finger.

Just like the link between the business cards from twenty years apart, she felt like there was something there...some clue just waiting for her to snatch it out of thin air.

The fact that it wouldn't come to her was maddening.

She slammed the folder shut and opened up the directory for headquarters. She had an idea of how to possibly pry the idea out of her but it was not going to be pretty. Back in Nebraska, she had caught a glimpse of a part of her that she thought she had buried. She had gone dark. *Going dark* was something she had done quite a bit of during her teenage years. She'd gotten violent and confused and had acted out on a few occasions.

And she feared that to get to the conclusion she was looking for, she just might have to touch upon some of those darker edges.

She found the number she was looking for in the directory and called it, finding that she was actually willing to explore the anger and hostility that had caused her to put a fist through the wall of her childhood home two days ago.

If she was being honest, a small part of her had missed it.

A small part of her had wanted it back for quite some time.

CHAPTER TWENTY SEVEN

Mackenzie balked a little at the sight of Dr. Madeline Goldsmith's office. It was sickeningly pretentious and looked like it had come out of some really bad Sunday night drama on primetime TV. She had met with Dr. Goldsmith twice upon coming to Quantico, as per the bureau's orders following her quick rise to fame after the Scarecrow Killer case—the case that had more or less put her on the map and led her to the FBI.

She'd gone to those two sessions only because they had been mandatory but had skirted them after that. It seemed to be something that Dr. Goldsmith almost held against her. Still, she had agreed to see Mackenzie that very day, scheduling in some time at 3:00, just an hour and a half after Mackenzie had called her.

Refusing to become a living cliché by sitting on the couch, Mackenzie stood by Dr. Goldsmith's window and looked out into DC. She saw a group of academy students filing out of a lecture hall and tried to remember what that had been like. It had been less than nine weeks ago but it seemed like forever.

"Why did you wait so long to speak with me, Mackenzie?" Goldsmith asked.

"I didn't see the need. No offense."

"You said that you think speaking with me might help you to tease out some clue to this case you're working on, correct?"

"Yes. I think I can be led to this one little item that I can't seem to latch onto with the right line of questioning."

"And you think I can do that for you?" Goldsmith asked.

"I do."

"Is that because of your reputation for being able to get into the minds of the people you are after? Do you think that if I can somehow get into your head and force you to speak about certain things, you might unwittingly discover the answer you're looking for?"

"Yes," Mackenzie said, a little uncomfortably.

"Okay," Goldsmith said. "That's a little unorthodox and not at all what I usually do, but let's give it a shot. Why don't you catch me up on what's been bothering you these last several days, aside from the obvious trials of the case."

Mackenzie spent the next fifteen minutes spelling out the Little Hill case and the tension between the state PD, the local PD, and the park rangers. She then told Goldsmith about her impromptu trip to Nebraska and how it had affected her. The only thing she left out was the devastating news that Bryers had given her. She was keeping that to herself for now.

"I want to start with you putting your fist through the wall of the room your father died in. What was that about?"

"I was frustrated."

"I need more than that, Mackenzie."

She looked to the hand she had sent through the wall and frowned. "That damn room has haunted me my entire life. To realize that as I was standing there a few days ago…it was my way of telling it to fuck off. I'm done with it. I can't let it affect me anymore."

"Are you *truly* done with it, though?"

"I'd like to be. I'd like to think so." *Aside from this lingering suspicion about my mother,* she thought but didn't dare say.

"And this connection between the new case and your father's case. Do you feel that it is, in a way, resurrecting the guilt you say you felt about your father's death?"

"No. I don't feel guilty about it. I haven't in a while. But there's that darkness I felt. It was me going dark again, like when I was an angry stupid teenager."

"Like dark thoughts?" Goldsmith asked.

"Yes, but more than that. It's like seeing the world through a lens of negativity and hatred. I have to sort of tap into it sometimes to get into the mind of a killer—to think like they do. And I haven't been able to do that yet with this case. Something seems off about it."

"Does it make you feel like an inadequate agent?"

Mackenzie thought about this for a moment and then shook her head slowly. "No. It makes me feel weak, though. I've got too much distracting me."

"Well, your work can't make up your entire life," Goldsmith said.

"I'm slowly finding that out," Mackenzie said. "But with this job, it can happen so easily."

"Is there anyone you can think of that could help you through this? Someone that can help you map out the intricacies of your life? A family member? A love interest?"

"No," Mackenzie said. "I've pretty much driven anyone that fills those roles away. All I really have right now is Bryers and he—"

She stopped here, thinking. It was more than wanting to keep Bryers's current health a secret; something had sparked in her. An idea. An inkling of a theory.

"What about Bryers?"

"Nothing," she said absently. Her mind was backtracking a bit, to something Goldsmith had said.

Someone that can help you map out the intricacies of your life...

"Mackenzie?"

"Hold on," she said, starting to pace around the room.

Maybe she had been unable to get into this killer's head because it wasn't a killer's head she was trying to step into. Maybe there was...well, maybe there was help.

But the word *help* wasn't what had created the spark in her mind. It was another word entirely: *map*.

"Did we do it?" Goldsmith said. "Did you stumble upon what you were looking for?"

Mackenzie nodded slowly.

She thought of Brian Woerner. He had gone out in Little Hill State Park despite the barricades. And then he had apparently been taken without a drone, park rangers, or manned police cars seeing him. What were the odds of that? Sure, he'd gotten into the park because he knew the grounds, but who else would have known where someone might sneak in? Who else would have known when it was safe to go after a curious passerby?

Who else could have *mapped* the area so perfectly?

"Shit," Mackenzie said. "I have to go. Thanks so much."

"Okay," Goldsmith said as Mackenzie made her way to the door. "But Mackenzie?"

"Yes?" she said, impatiently.

"Don't wait so long to see me again?"

Mackenzie only responded with a nod. Before the door was even closed behind her, she pulled out her phone and called Bryers. He answered on the second ring and sounded a little tired. He sounded like he had been coughing a lot lately.

"You said you wanted to be of use before you kicked off, right?" Mackenzie asked.

"Yeah. Why?"

"I think I have an idea. I think I might know who's been orchestrating the deaths at Little Hill."

"Who?"

"Do you have any idea who was posted closest to where Brian Woerner snuck into the park?" she asked.

"Um...yeah, I'm pretty sure it was one of your good friends, the park rangers."

"Can you be ready to leave for Strasburg in ten minutes?" Mackenzie asked.

"I can be ready in five," he said, no longer sounding tired.

Mackenzie hurried down to the parking garage, confident that this would be the last God-awful trip to Strasburg she would have to make.

CHAPTER TWENTY EIGHT

When Mackenzie pulled her car into the small parking lot of the Strasburg police station, Clements and Smith were already waiting. Dusk was approaching, settling quietly over the little town. Smith gave a little wave as they stepped out of the car. Clements, on the other hand, did not look happy. He approached them like a soldier marching to war, his jaw set and his eyes narrowed.

"Are you *certain* about this?" Clements asked.

"Like I told you on the phone," Mackenzie said, "I'm not absolutely certain but everything points to it. And the worst thing that could happen is that we end up with a very pissed off park ranger when all is said and done."

"Holt," Clements said, shaking his head. "Charlie Holt of all people. You think he did it?"

"I don't know," Mackenzie repeated, almost as if she were speaking to a five-year-old. "But I think we need to look into it."

"We still have to be careful about how we approach this," Smith said. "You're accusing a state park ranger of some pretty heinous acts."

"The thing is," Clements said, "I almost find it easy to believe. Holt always sort of seemed like an odd duck, you know? Staring out into space all the time, sort of muttering to himself. Always picking at those acorns like a druggie jonesing for a fix."

"I picked up on that," Mackenzie said. "The fixation on the acorns shows that he was nervous about something. Looking back on it, it was more than just a compulsive thing like smoking when a smoker gets nervous. He was fidgeting...he was occupying his hands, like he was afraid he might literally jump out of his skin."

"Were you able to pull his records?" Bryers asked Clements.

"Yeah," Clements said. He offered Mackenzie a folder he had been holding in his hands the entire time.

Mackenzie looked it over quickly, looking for anything that stood out to her. Charlie Holt was twenty-seven years old and had gotten the job as a ranger thanks to an agriculture degree from Virginia Tech. He'd started two years ago as a guide for youth-oriented park programs and had eventually been given security patrol before coming on as a ranger one year later. He had no criminal record but there were also no references other than a few from college.

"There's nothing from before college?" she asked. "No high school information or anything?" Mackenzie asked.

"No," Clements said. "But why does that matter?"

"Do we know where he grew up? Where did he live before he went to Virginia Tech?"

"Not sure," Clements said. "I'm pretty sure the applications to work as a ranger don't require much of anything other than a basic background check and college information. And from what I can tell, he's clean."

Silence fell among the four of them—a silence that didn't end until Clements kicked at the tire of his patrol car and said, "Ah, hell. Let's get it over with. But not all four of us. If we go after him and we're wrong, I don't want it to seem like we're bullying him."

"Just you and me then," Mackenzie said. "In and out, really quick. It'll be like pulling off a Band-Aid."

"For you, maybe," Clements said. "If we're wrong on this, I'll have to face the backlash."

Mackenzie understood his concern, but she also felt that her hunch was right. To know the woods so well, to know when the drones were going out...it was either a local cop or a ranger. And based on the way Charlie Holt had reacted when the FBI had come in *and* his position along the perimeter on the day Brian Woerner got through, he was certainly worth checking out. The fact that he had such a blank space in his record also made her feel that he was a prime candidate.

It was a certainty that felt solid as she got into the passenger seat of Clements's patrol car. As they pulled out, she watched Bryers walk inside the station with Smith and felt that they needed to act fast. Something about Bryers filling her in on his limited time to live had her feeling as if her time was running out, too.

***

Charlie Holt lived in a ramshackle one-story house on the east edge of Strasburg. It was a lower-middle-class neighborhood with tall grass and cracked sidewalks. It was less than a twenty-minute drive from Little Hill and when Clements parked the car, night had fallen completely. Mackenzie found it almost comforting that they were able to simply walk right up to Charlie's front door and knock. It was that sort of community—quiet, with streetlights on every corner with no real need to feel secure.

Clements knocked on the door. Mackenzie made sure to step back in order to seem less intimidating. She recalled Charlie's reaction to her presence on that first crime scene. If he felt that she was running things, he might not talk at all. But if she could take a back seat—if she could even maybe seem subservient to Clements—that might be her best bet.

Charlie answered several seconds later. He opened the door about halfway and Mackenzie took note of his expression when he saw who was on his front porch. At first there was confusion and then a flash of fear. She watched his eyes closely, knowing that eyes that shifted nervously usually indicated either guilt or that the subject was hiding something. With Charlie Holt, she saw that telltale sign quite easily. He was absolutely hiding something and he was not happy that the local police chief and an FBI agent were paying him a visit.

"Charlie," Clements said, "I'd like to ask you some questions about the mess going on in Little Hill. You think that would be okay?"

Charlie didn't answer right away. He shifted his eyes again, this time looking to the floor. "I guess," he said hesitantly. "Come on in. But…well, why is *she* here?"

"Because it's a federal case," Mackenzie asked. "My being here eliminates a middleman and speeds up communication. Nothing big."

"She's right," Clements said. "We just have a few basic questions to ask."

Charlie led them into his house. The TV was tuned to *Wheel of Fortune* and a plate of mac and cheese and cut up hot dogs was sitting on the sofa. Mackenzie saw all of this but she also noticed that Charlie picked up his cell phone from the small coffee table and pocketed it right away. He did it quickly, as if trying to hide it.

"So, you know that a local guy is missing now," Clements said. "Brian Woerner."

"Yes, I know."

"We were wondering how he got into the park at all with the cops and rangers blocking the roads," Clements said. "Any ideas on that?"

"None," Charlie said. "Some of these local kids know the woods just about as well as I do. He probably used to neck down there with some girl. Or get stoned, or something."

"Probably," Clements said. "Charlie, do you know who was supposed to be monitoring the road that Woerner was able to access the park from?"

Mackenzie listened to all of this as she took in the rest of the living room. She did not want to scour the house without his permission. As it was, Clements was questioning him pretty aggressively; Mackenzie did not want to give him another reason to freak out prematurely. He was guilty of *something* and she hoped to find out without things getting nasty.

"I don't know," Charlie said, finally answering the last question. "Andrews, maybe?"

"It wasn't you?" Clements asked.

"No. I was…ah, hell, I forget. I was down by the water station most of the day, protecting that road."

"Oh, okay," Clements said. He gave Mackenzie a brief glance that told her that this was a lie. He frowned slightly, knowing what they were going to have to do.

Mackenzie stepped forward then. While she did not agree with the way Clements was approaching his interrogation, she knew she had to stick with it. Good cop/bad cop only worked in the movies. In reality, it was consistency that usually got results.

"Charlie, can I please see your phone?" she asked.

"What phone?"

"The one I watched you slip into your pocket like some magician when we came in."

"What for?" Charlie asked.

"Just to check something. You seemed anxious to get it out of our sight."

"You need a warrant for that, don't you?" Charlie asked.

"Damn, Charlie," Clements said. "Just let her see your phone."

"No. It's none of her business."

"If I have to get a warrant, I will," Mackenzie said. "Or you can save me the trouble and an obstruction charge by just handing it over and—"

She was interrupted mid-sentence as Charlie reached out, grabbed his plate of mac and cheese and hot dogs, and threw it like a Frisbee.

Clements had just enough time to let out a quick "*What the fu—*" before it hit him in the face.

It took exactly two seconds for Mackenzie to move. Charlie had already bolted for the back of the house. His footfalls thundered through the place like a herd of cows. Mackenzie went after him, unsure if he was attempting an escape or making a dash for a weapon.

She followed him into a small hallway that led to a small kitchen. Beyond it, she could see a back door and the night waiting outside. Charlie was heading for the back door, apparently thinking he could escape.

From behind her, Mackenzie heard Clements scream out Charlie's name in primal rage. She ignored it, though. Charlie was fast but he was also jittery and scared. He made it into the kitchen but as he turned and headed for the back door, Mackenzie dropped low and launched herself at his knees.

She hit him dead-on, taking his legs out. He toppled over, striking his head on the edge of the kitchen counter. Mackenzie came up out of a roll, bouncing hard off of a row of cabinets along the floor. She then dove on Charlie before he had time to even figure out what had happened.

Mackenzie planted a knee in his back and pulled his arms behind him. In that instant, Clements came rushing into the kitchen. He nearly pushed Mackenzie off of Charlie so that he could slap a set of handcuffs on him.

"Get on your fucking feet," Clements muttered. He yanked Charlie up and pushed him hard against the counter.

Mackenzie did her best to look away from Clements. There was macaroni and cheese in his hair and smeared on his face. A chunk of hot dog was trapped between his neck and the collar of his shirt.

"Charlie, you're under arrest," Clements seethed. He then turned to Mackenzie and said, "If you tell anyone about this, I'll kill you. And if I can't kill you, I'll kill myself."

He grinned in spite of himself and plucked the piece of hotdog away from his neck.

"Your secret is safe with me," she said. She stepped forward and reached into Charlie's pocket. She took out the phone and showed it to Charlie.

"What's your password?"

Charlie shook his head in response.

Mackenzie shrugged. "It doesn't matter. We can have someone crack it within an hour. In the meantime, I think we need to have a little talk."

CHAPTER TWENTY NINE

The interrogation room inside the Strasburg PD wasn't much but something about it actually fed into Mackenzie's mood. It was small, confined, and dimly lit. It smelled of old cigarette smoke and sweat. A single camera sat in the upper left corner of the room, recording the session and relaying it to a small TV in a viewing room down the hall. Because the room was so small and closed off—not much more than a large walk-in closet, really—it was a bit warmer than the rest of the building.

Charlie Holt sat at the small table in the center of the room. He looked nervous and even a bit scared. He'd tried the tough guy act in the car on the way to the police department but it had crumbled away as soon as he had been led into the interrogation room. Despite this, he was refusing to talk. He would not respond to even the simplest, most basic of questions.

There was only one chair in the room, and Charlie Holt was sitting in it. Mackenzie stood with her back against the wall, eyeing him closely and trying to figure him out.

"Charlie…throwing your dinner at a police officer shows either some sort of mental imbalance or a degree of guilt. You understand why we're suspicious, right?"

Charlie said nothing. He only looked at her fleetingly, in the same way he had on the first day she and Bryers had come onto the case.

"The longer you stay quiet, the more suspicious you seem," she went on. "More than that, if you don't give me some answers, I'm going to give up and let Sheriff Clements come in here and question you. And trust me…he's still plenty pissed and embarrassed about what happened. Given the circumstances, I think you'd rather have me to speak to."

Charlie opened his mouth to say something but then bit it back at the last moment. He shook his head and said: "I'm not talking."

"And why is that, Charlie?" she said. "What is it that you *don't* want to talk about? The murders?"

His eyes went to the table and his entire body seemed to go rigid. He was scared, all right. But Mackenzie thought there might be something else going on. He was scared…but not of her. He was afraid of saying something he shouldn't but his body language and reaction made her think it was more than spilling his secrets that he was worried about. She'd seen this sort of thing before during her academy training and a few times on a smaller scale when she'd been working as a detective in Nebraska.

"You know where Brian Woerner is, don't you?" Mackenzie said.

He remained silent.

"How much strength does it take to sever a leg at the knee?" she asked, hoping to jar him into an admission. "And what did you use to make such a fairly clean cut, even through the bone?"

He held his silence but started to squirm uncomfortably in his chair. She studied him, watching his face and narrowing in on his eyes. He was scared, upset...but something else. He was certainly hiding something but she didn't think it was something *he* had done. The reaction to her violent descriptions and his utter refusal to talk at all made her think that something strange was at play here.

An idea so profound popped into her head that she stood up from the wall in a hurry.

The blank spot in his records...nothing before college...

She walked closer to the table and stayed quiet. She simply studied Charlie's face for a moment and saw all she needed to see. Just in case, though, she added one more question.

"You didn't kill those people, did you?"

He looked at her for a moment...a quick second at best. But it was all she needed to see. There was relief there. There was truth there. And there was...well, there was something else, too.

He's not our guy at all. Well, he's not the killer, *anyway. If I'm right on this...oh my God...*

"I'll be right back, Charlie."

Mackenzie left the interrogation room, closing the door tightly behind her, and headed to the next room down the hall. She joined Bryers, Clements, and Smith, all huddled around the small TV bolted to the wall.

"Let me talk to him," Clements said.

"Not just yet," Mackenzie said. "Smith, do you recall the specifics of the Will Albrecht abduction?"

"Most of them. What do you need to know?"

"Will was how old when he was taken?"

"Seven," Smith answered. "A month shy of being eight."

"Taken nineteen years ago?" Mackenzie asked.

"Yes," Smith said. "Why do you...no. *No way.*"

"Will Albrecht would have been twenty-seven years old today. Charlie Holt is twenty-seven years old. He also has a record that has quite a few missing years prior to college."

"That's one hell of a stretch," Clements said.

"Is it?" Bryers asked. "Let's find out."

He pulled out his cell phone and placed a call. He walked to the back of the room to speak to the person on the other line. He murmured quietly as a thick wave of tension started to fill the room.

"Just let me get this straight," Clements said. "You expect me to believe that Will Albrecht survived his abduction and then came back to his hometown without anyone realizing it was him? Not only that, but that he took a job as a park ranger and is now killing people?"

"You're partly right," she said. "You know as well as I do that his family moved away after the abduction. So there's no family here that would recognize him. I don't think he came back. I don't think he ever left."

He stared at her.

"What are you saying?" he asked.

She sighed.

"I don't think he's killing these people," she said. "But I think he's *helping*."

"Helping who?" Clements asked, clearly not understanding.

Mackenzie stared back.

"The psycho who abducted him twenty years ago."

They all stared back at her, clearly processing it, as a heavy silence blanketed the room.

"He's showing textbook signs of protecting someone," Mackenzie continued. "He's not worried about spilling his own secrets. He seems more worried about slipping up and saying something he's not supposed to. And that almost certainly indicates that there is someone else involved. And whenever I direct the questions to the gruesome nature of the crimes, he gets visibly uncomfortable."

While Clements and Smith mulled this over (Smith with an impressed smile on his face), Bryers joined them again. "I've got Intelligence working to pull a birth certificate for Charlie Holt, Virginia Tech graduate and current employee at Little Hill State Park. We should have results pretty soon."

Clements stared at the television screen with his hands on his hips.

"Unbelievable," he said. "If this turns out to be true..."

"I want to wait for the call from Intelligence," Mackenzie said. "I want to know for absolutely sure if this turns out before speaking with him again. He's scared and sort of fragile right now. If I can use this as a weapon, he'll crumble pretty easily, I think."

137

"But what if he *is* the killer?" Smith asked. "I mean...did we get him just like that? Is it over that easily?"

It was a pleasant thought but Mackenzie was nearly certain Charlie Holt (if that was his name, something she doubted very strongly) was not a killer. With the way the bodies had been slaughtered and nearly put on some weird sort of display, the killer would likely be very proud and boastful about this work...not cowering and close to tears.

Mackenzie watched him on the television. He couldn't seem to get comfortable in his chair. On one occasion, he turned and looked to the camera, as if he could feel their eyes on him from the next room.

Behind her, everyone else milled around anxiously. Smith stepped out for a coffee. Clements went out to check on a few smaller matters in his office. Bryers stayed by her side but remained quiet. She felt him back behind her like a ghost...and given his current condition, it was something of an eerie feeling.

She wasn't sure how much time had passed when Bryers's phone rang. He answered it quickly and Mackenzie did her best to listen in as Bryers gave a series of *Yeah*s and *Thank you*s. When he ended the call a minute later, he looked a little grave yet resigned.

"There's no record on Charlie Holt prior to middle school," he said. "He attended Barnes Middle School and the Barnes High School in Pennsylvania. Before that, though...nothing. No record of a birth certificate. No immunization records before middle school. And the only emergency contact Intelligence could find is a Bob White...deceased in 2011. Another thing to note is that there's some question over the authenticity of the middle school records."

"Are they fakes?"

"I'm not sure. The guys at Intelligence are looking into it. Still, I think it's something of a stretch to say that Charlie Holt is Will Albrecht."

Mackenzie wasn't so sure.

"Only one way to find out," she said.

CHAPTER THIRTY

When Mackenzie stepped back into the interrogation room, she was very aware of the three sets of eyes that were watching her through the camera. She was also very aware of the distrustful look on Charlie's face.

"This is your last chance," Mackenzie said. "You talk now or you're going to spend some time in jail." This, she knew, was not accurate unless they could pin something on him—but she was pretty sure he wouldn't know such a thing.

Charlie only shrugged.

"Why did you try to run when we came by just to ask you some questions about the case? As a park ranger, you should have been more than willing to help."

He stayed quiet. Mackenzie almost wished he would do it defiantly. Maybe with his arms crossed or with a sly grin on his face. But no…Charlie was shaking in his boots, his lips quivering and his eyes on the verge of welling with tears.

"Fine. Stay quiet," she said. "But in the meantime, I want to tell you a story. Is that okay?" Without giving him time to understand what she meant, Mackenzie started: "While the grisly murders in Little Hill State Park are certainly tragic, it's worth noting that it's not the first time something terrible has happened in the park. You see…about twenty years ago, a little boy went missing. He was seven years old and was abducted right off the trails when he got ahead of his parents on his bike. The police searched and searched but the kid never turned up."

Mackenzie paused here, leaning on the edge of the table and looking directly into his eyes. A tear finally spilled down his cheek, and then another. He let out a pitiful little moan and looked away from her.

"The story continues with a park ranger that has worked at Little Hill for a few years now. He's a nice enough guy but the funny thing is that when the police started looking back into his history, there's a big chunk missing. There's no record of him ever being a kid—not before attending middle school in Pennsylvania anyway. And then there's—"

"Stop," he said. "Just *stop!*" He sniffled and looked up to her again. He looked lost. He looked defeated and broken.

Mackenzie stepped away from the table, just a few steps, to not seem so threatening. She then sighed and put on a soft, reassuring tone.

"Where were you all of those years, Will?"

"He was taking care of me."

"Who?"

Will Albrecht shook his head. It was the first time he had seemed absolutely unwilling to cooperate. His jaw was clenched and his eyes, while still spilling tears, were ice cold.

"Let me see if I can connect the dots for you," she said. "I think there's a chance that you were abducted and then cared for by whoever took you. Maybe the two of you left the area and lived a secret life somewhere else. Pennsylvania, perhaps. And then you come back here with your abductor. You take on a job as a park ranger so that you can...what? Help him find his next victims?"

He looked up to her with a strange look that was like some sort of pleading rage. "It's not like that. He's...he's helping—"

"Who? And why on God's green earth have you been helping?"

He shook his head again.

"How do you do it, Will? How do you select the people this man kills? What made Brian Woerner a candidate? Will...you know who the killer is, don't you? You've been helping him."

"I...had to. It's important. What he's doing...so important. And he...he would hurt me."

"Will...whether he thinks it's important or not, it's wrong. He's killing people. He's *butchering* them. And you're *assisting him*!"

He just shook his head, silent.

"You have to tell us who it is," Mackenzie said. "You have to help us find him."

But he remained silent.

She felt anger flaring up, felt the darkness wanting to rush in and take over. But she had finally gotten through to him. She knew the make-up of this sort of person; he'd been stolen and then effectively brainwashed by his captor. If she lost her temper with him, he'd shut down completely.

"Put me in jail if you need to," he said. He was still weeping, but his voice was calm. Almost at peace. "Do anything you feel you have to do. But I am not going to talk anymore."

She knew she had to step away. She'd already blown his cover and spoiled his fake identity. She had, in a very skewed way, upended his life in that moment. After such a traumatic event, she knew that he was not likely to give up anything else. With his cover blown, what else did he have to lose? Just one thing,

140

apparently…the identity of the killer. And she was pretty sure he would hold on to that for dear life.

"Fine, Will," she said. "But I want you to think about it long and hard. I want you to think about the scenes you have seen out in the forests…the work of the man you are protecting. The blood he has spilled and the sorrow he has caused is on your hands, too. You can make amends for it by doing the right thing."

Again, Will Albrecht shook his head.

Slowly, Mackenzie headed back toward the door. She exited the interrogation room and when she was back outside in the hallway, she started clenching and unclenching her fists. Anger and logic were doing battle and in that moment, she didn't honestly care which one came out the victor.

Clements came rushing to meet her. His eyes were wild with excitement.

"Holy shit," he said. "You were right."

"But there's still a killer out there," she said, "and if Will doesn't talk, we're no closer to finding him."

From inside her pocket, her phone buzzed. She slid it out and looked at the display.

It was McGrath.

Her heart dropped in her chest as she wondered what he might be calling about. Instantly, she thought about her trip to Nebraska and how she had lied to him about the reasons behind it.

"Sorry," she said to Clements. "I have to take this."

She stepped away, took a deep breath, and then answered. "This is Agent White."

"Mackenzie," he said. "Are you in Strasburg?"

"Yes, sir. What's up?"

"Just wanted to make sure since you apparently have a habit of lying to your superiors about why you are traveling certain places."

"Sir, I—"

"Shut up. For once, be quiet, White. I've got one hell of a bone to pick with you."

CHAPTER THIRTY ONE

"I'm listening," she said. She hated that she was instantly nervous. She had a feeling she knew what this was about and figured she deserved whatever consequence came her way.

"Your trip to Nebraska," he said. "I have it on good authority that you were not completely honest with me. Do you want to come clean now or am I going to have to lecture and berate you?"

She didn't see the point in lying or even hesitating. "Something happened down there. A new case that links to my father's case. A PI down there clued me in to it. Sir…I don't even know if I can explain why, but I had to check it out for myself before it landed on the desk of someone at the bureau."

"And why is that?" McGrath asked.

"Because I knew the chances of me getting any sort of play on it were very slim. I had to have a look before I was basically shut off from it."

McGrath was silent for a while and when he spoke again, his words came out slow and calculated. "I understand your need to look into it yourself. But if you ever lie to me again in such a way, I'll make sure that you are stripped of your badge."

"Yes, sir."

He sighed, and a long pause followed. Mackenzie felt her heart thumping, wondering if she would lose her job before she even started.

"Look," he finally said, his tone softened. "I'm sure I'll regret this later but I'll tell you what: you wrap this thing up with a nice bow before another body turns up and I'll see what I can do about getting you on the case. It has, by the way, officially come through. As of tomorrow, it's an active case. And if I put you on it, you have to keep a low profile…so don't get too excited just yet."

"Thank you, sir."

"Don't thank me yet. For now, just go out there and round us up this Campground Killer."

He killed the call before she had time to give him any assurances. She pocketed her phone and walked quickly to the small break room. Smith and Bryers were sitting at a little table, sipping from Styrofoam cups of coffee. Mackenzie grabbed her own and then joined them.

"Smith," she said, "I wonder if you'd do me a favor and let Bryers and I speak in private?"

Smith nodded and took his leave. He seemed almost happy to do so. He looked restless and tired as he made his exit.

"Everything okay?" Bryers asked as Mackenzie took her seat.

"Well, things are *weird,*" she said. "McGrath just called me. I don't know how, but he somehow found out why I went back to Nebraska."

"You think it was the PI you met with?"

"I can't be sure, but I really don't think so. But I can't figure any other way he would have known."

"Was he pissed?" Bryers asked.

"That's just the thing," Mackenzie said. "He certainly wasn't happy about it, but he wasn't nearly as upset as he usually is over insubordination. He even told me he'd put me on the case if I wanted it. But I had to be discreet about it."

"That's amazing," Bryers said. "When is he sending you out there?"

She shrugged and sighed. "I don't know if I'm going to take it."

"Why wouldn't you?" he asked.

"Because that's a part of my past. A past I've spent my entire life trying to escape. This case feels like an undertow...pulling me back. And while part of me very badly wants to get back out there and figure out the connection to my father...the smarter part of me tells me to leave it alone."

What she didn't add was the harrowing thought that she had managed to get by just fine without the guidance or support of the rest of her family—why would leaving behind the mystery of her father's death be any different?

There was, of course, the new revelations with her mother to be considered.

"That's pretty remarkable of you," Bryers said. "And if I may be so blunt, I think it's the smartest decision. Nebraska and everything that happened there is in your past. What you're doing now...well, it's your present *and* your future. You're damned good at what you do, Mac. I'm still floored at how you figured out Charlie Holt was really Will Albrecht. Never let your past pull you down or prevent you from going forward." He stopped here and gave her a weak smile. "Take it from a dying man that doesn't have time to fully appreciate his future."

"Bryers, you can't think like that," she said. "It's defeatist. It's—"

A knock at the door interrupted her. Clements opened the door and stepped inside. He looked almost apologetic, as if he knew he was breaking up something important.

"Sorry to interrupt," he said. "But we're going to go ahead and put Albrecht in a cell for the night. Maybe he'll talk tomorrow."

"Maybe," Mackenzie said. She couldn't help but notice the shift in his demeanor. He had been a totally different man four days ago when she and Bryers had first walked in on the case. She wondered if it had been her effectiveness or the nature of the escalating case that had changed his demeanor.

"So you're okay with us locking him up?" he asked.

"I think you have more than enough reason," Mackenzie said. "I also think it might not hurt to send a few people over to his house to see if there's anything there worth looking at. Will is our best bet to find this killer—and he may be our only chance."

Clements nodded, gave a quick and gruff "Thanks" and then headed back out of the room.

When he was gone, Bryers got to his feet and stretched.

"Damn good work tonight, Mac," he said. "How about we head on back to the motel and get some shut-eye? With Albrecht in a cell, there's nothing much else we can do here until he decides to talk."

She wanted to hang out to potentially question Will Albrecht some more. Surely he'd crack at some point. But she could leave instructions with Clements and his local boys to call her if that happened. For now, Bryers was right. She needed to sleep. She needed to recharge.

Bryers let out a mighty whooping cough that jarred Mackenzie to her bones. She frowned at him and, as a means to skimp on the nurturing sympathy she knew would make him uncomfortable, she shook her head.

"Jeez, Bryers," she said. "You sound awful. I'm driving."

She could see in his eyes that he appreciated the light-heartedness. "Probably a good idea," he said.

She opened the door for him but kept her eyes to the floor, afraid her emotions might betray her that she'd start crying at any moment.

***

Although she was exhausted, Mackenzie lay in the darkness of her motel room and stared at the dark ceiling, unable to find sleep. She tried her best to keep her mind on the Little Hill case but images of that damned business card popped into her head again and again.

Barker Antiques, she thought. *A place that apparently doesn't even exist. What the hell?*

In many ways, the inclusion of the business cards at the scenes of the deaths of her father and of Jimmy Scotts was very similar to what the killer was doing at Little Hill. He was butchering his victims and putting them on display. He *wanted* people to see the shape of the bodies. And the person leaving the business cards *wanted* to leave the clues in a subtle yet daring way.

But why?

With no answer to this question forthcoming, Mackenzie finally allowed herself the gift of sleep. She dreamed, but not the usual nightmare that plagued her. In this dream, she was standing in a house that she had never been in before but was filled with familiar shapes and angles. She held a sledgehammer in her hands and was tearing into the walls. Plaster came down like snow all around her. As she tore into yet another wall, she could see into the room beyond it. In it, she could Stephanie. She was screaming into a phone and although Mackenzie's dream-self had no way of knowing this, she was certain that their mother was on the other end.

Stephanie saw Mackenzie looking through the jagged hole in the wall and came dashing to it. She held the phone out to Mackenzie with tears in her eyes.

"She wants to talk to you," Stephanie said.

Mackenzie reached through the hole and took the phone.

That's when she jerked awake in bed. She heard a phone ringing but was somehow sure that it was connected to the dream. But the familiar sounds of her basic ringtone coming from her phone finally pulled her completely out of sleep.

As she grabbed her cell phone from the bedside table, her sleep-smeared eyes took in the digital numbers on the alarm clock. 3:56.

She answered the call and didn't do much to disguise the fact that she had just been torn from sleep. "Hello," she said without opening her mouth much.

"Agent White?"

"Yeah. Who's this?"

"It's Clements," came the sheriff's voice. "Sorry to call at such a crazy hour, but I think you might want to get down to the Strasburg PD."

"Why? What's up?"

"It's Charlie Holt…or Will Albrecht, I guess."

"What about him?" Mackenzie asked.

"He killed himself."

CHAPTER THIRTY TWO

She arrived at the station, sans makeup or coffee, at 4:18. She was sure she'd catch hell from Bryers, but she had not called him. She wanted him to get his rest. Besides that, there really wasn't much that they could do now that Albrecht had killed himself. No sense in stealing any of Bryers's much-needed rest.

An ambulance was parked in the lot, just in front of the doors. The red lights on the roof were flashing, painting everything red.

Clements met her at the door, looking just as tired as she was. He had two cups of coffee in his hands, one of which he handed to Mackenzie.

"Where's your partner?" he asked.

"I let him sleep," she said, graciously accepting the coffee. "Nothing two people can do for a suicide that one can't. How'd he do it?" she asked.

"Wrapped a bed sheet around his neck and hung himself. The medics damn near brought him back but we lost him about two minutes before I called you."

He led her to the back of the building where there were three small holding cells. They consisted of bare concrete floors, a single cot, and a small table by the cot. The first one they came to was occupied by two paramedics and a dead body covered with a sheet on a gurney.

Mackenzie looked inside, confused. "How the hell did he manage to hang himself in there?"

One of the paramedics shook her head and said, "He didn't *hang* himself per se. He choked himself. Tied one end of the sheet around his neck in some expert Boy Scout knot and the other to the foot of the cot. The cot is bolted to the wall so when he got on the floor and pulled forward, it didn't budge."

"That takes some determination," Mackenzie said.

"You can say that again," the paramedic said as they wheeled the gurney out of the cell. "You need the body for anything?"

"No," Mackenzie said, disappointed. "I'm good."

She then couldn't help but wonder: *What if he was the killer? What if the killer was caught, killed himself, and this case is over?*

She wanted to feel relief at the thought but it wasn't there. She knew Charlie/Will was not the killer. She just hoped it was a realization that Clements and Smith would also see.

"Sorry about this," Clements said. "We don't exactly keep security cameras on the cells or guards stationed outside of them. In a small city like this—"

"I know," Mackenzie said. "And don't be sorry. There's no way you could have known."

They walked to the small break room where the smell of freshly brewed coffee made Mackenzie realize that her first cup was nearly gone.

"So what now?" Clements asked. "If your theory is right and he was only working for someone was not the killer, this is a big setback, right?"

"Yes. But listen to me, Clements. The killer—the way he disposed of the bodies—speaks of arrogance. He wanted us to see his work. If Will Albrecht was indeed the killer, he would not have killed himself before confessing…maybe even boasting or bragging."

"Are you sure?" he asked.

"Almost positive," she replied. "He was *really* scared of saying the wrong thing…afraid he might say something incriminating. Did he say anything at all the rest of the night?"

"Nothing," Clements said. "The only time I saw a single sign of life out of him was when we took his personal belongings from his pockets. We checked him right away when you and I brought him in, of course. No weapons on him. But when we tried taking those acorns out of his pockets and out of his hands right after you and your partner left, he lost his shit."

The acorns, Mackenzie thought. She then thought of the business cards from the two cases in Nebraska. They had been left behind as a taunt of sorts. But in the end, when all was said and done, it was an identifier of sorts.

Maybe the acorns can be an identifier, too. There were no prints, no signs of struggle or abduction. But maybe the acorns are a clue in and of themselves.

"Where did the acorns end up?" she asked.

Clements shrugged. "Probably in the trash. I can check with the officer on duty that took them from him. He's still here."

"I think I'd like to speak to him, please."

"Sure thing. Come on."

Clements led her to the front of the building where a bored receptionist sat behind a desk, scanning a magazine. Two officers stood against the far wall. One was reading over a report of some kind while the other one spoke to him.

"Hey, Gary," Clements said.

148

The cop holding the report looked up and came over when Clements beckoned him forward.

"When you took the acorns from Albrecht, was there anything else in his pockets?" Clements asked.

"Nope. Just lint and dirt."

"How many acorns were there?" Mackenzie asked.

"I don't remember. But they're still bagged and in the evidence locker if you want to see them."

"Thanks," Mackenzie said. "Clements, can you get that bag for me? And what was the name of the other ranger that was at the first scene with us?"

"Joe Andrews."

"Can you get him down here?"

"That shouldn't be a problem," he said. "You got an idea or something?"

"Just a hunch," she said.

But the truth of the matter was that she *hoped* it might be much more than a hunch. She just had to hope that luck was on her side.

Charlie Holt/Will Albrecht picked those acorns up from the ground from somewhere within the park, she thought. *What if the acorns can tell us where he had been...acting like footprints in a way?*

As she followed Clements to the back of the police station, she pulled out her cell phone. It seemed like she was going to have to wake Bryers up after all. She called him and woke him up, filling him in on what had happened while she continued to follow Clements. She also told him one of the officers would arrive soon to pick him up and bring him to the station.

At the evidence locker, Clements unlocked it with a key from a chain on his belt. There were six acorns inside a clear plastic bag. One of them had been stripped nearly to its core. Mackenzie held the bag up to the light. Looking at the acorns, she saw that luck might be on her side after all.

Five of the acorns looked basically the same in appearance (except for the one stripped of its skin). But the sixth one looked different somehow. She knew nothing about trees but she was pretty sure the sixth one was different because it had come from a different tree.

While it could mean absolutely nothing, she had a feeling it might be a very big clue.

Over the course of the next half hour, Clements made sure his little conference room was cleaned and that the coffee was brewing. A few calls were made and Mackenzie did her best to compose herself. The night had been insane…hell, the last three or four days had been nuts. She felt herself slowly unraveling and did everything she could to stop it before it got any worse.

When Bryers arrived at the station fifteen minutes later, he was understandably irritated but not mad. He gave Mackenzie a slight nod of appreciation as he entered the conference room, where a handful of people had gathered. He took a seat to Mackenzie's left while Clements sat to her right with the evidence bag of acorns. Across the table, Joe Andrews held a white plastic bag he had brought with him.

Clements had informed Andrews of not only his co-worker's real identity, but of his suicide as well. Andrews was in an obvious state of shock. Even as they started their impromptu meeting, he seemed very much out of it.

"So," Clements said. "Why do we care about the acorns?"

Mackenzie took the bag from Clements. In it were the six acorns that had been taken from Will Albrecht's right pants pocket as well as the fragments of a few shells. She then took the bag that Joe Andrews had brought. There were fifteen acorns in that bag, all of which Andrews had taken from Will's locker at work.

Twenty-one acorns in all. She hoped there might be an answer to be found in at least one of them.

"You said yourself that he was always picking them up and peeling them or sticking them in his pockets, right?" Mackenzie asked.

"Yeah," Clements said. "He just had to fidget or something."

"Him and those acorns," Andrews said. "He was always picking them up. Sometimes I don't even think he knew he was doing it. His pockets were always full of them. He'd just pick them up and peel them—almost like he was going to eat them. I always thought it was sort of weird."

"That compulsive behavior is common among people with high anxiety or some form of trauma within their lives. But I wonder…Mr. Andrews, how much do you know about the forests out in the park?"

"In terms of animals and the river, quite a bit. But I'm guessing you want to know more about acorns, huh?"

"Yes. In particular, I'm wondering about the one in the evidence bag that looked to be different than the others."

"Hold on," Clements said. "Look…do we really want to delve into a study of acorns? I still think this is closed. This case…done. We caught the guy and he killed himself. I understand your theories and deductions, Agent White. I really do. But this is a waste of our time."

"Sheriff, you have to think about— "

"No," Clements said. "I really don't. You've kept me up far too late and I really am not interested in wasting any more time on this. If you want to go hunting for acorns out in the woods, that's your choice. But I'm not wasting any more of my time on it." He then got to his feet and looked back to her as he headed for the door. "You're welcome to finish your acorn study in my conference room. I'll give you five more minutes and then I'm going to politely ask you to leave—and to leave my overworked men out of it."

He took his exit, leaving Mackenzie, Bryers, and Joe Andrews in an uncomfortable silence.

"Well, that was a little dramatic," Bryers said.

"It was," Mackenzie agreed. "Mr. Andrews, you were saying?"

"I was saying that I can't really help you with any in-depth knowledge on acorns, but we have an agriculture expert at the park with a background in botany. Any question you have about trees or seeds, he's your man."

"How soon can I speak to him?"

"I'll get him on the phone right now," Andrews said, pulling out his cell phone. "But I've got to warn you...he's a little eccentric."

"Given my last few days, I'd welcome someone eccentric," Mackenzie said.

CHAPTER THIRTY THREE

The park ranger with a background in botany and agriculture was an older man—about sixty or so—with a thick moustache and a pair of glasses that looked like they'd been formed from the bottoms of glass bottles. His name was Barry D'Amour and he looked a little too happy to have been called in to work at six in the morning. He was already at work behind a laptop when Mackenzie and Bryers entered his office. Mackenzie carried the plastic bag of acorns Andrews had brought, complete with the six acorns that had been taken from Will Albrecht's pockets.

"Ah, Agents White and Bryers, I take it?" D'Amour said as they walked in.

"Yes," Mackenzie said. "Thanks for meeting with us so early. And at the risk of seeming unappreciative, we were hoping we could make this quick. If we can get results out of this, we could potentially unravel a new aspect of this case."

"Certainly," D'Amour said. He made a quick business of removing the clutter from his desk: the laptop, a few notebooks, pens, and scattered papers. The only thing remaining on his desk when he was done was a small lamp.

"Are those the acorns in question?" D'Amour asked.

"Yes," Mackenzie said, handing them over.

D'Amour peeked inside, grinned in an almost boyish fashion, and slowly dumped the twenty-one acorns out onto the table. When they were on the table, he worked quickly to align them in rows and piles. As he worked, he looked up to Mackenzie for a moment and asked: "What am I looking for?"

"Well, I noticed that there was one acorn in the evidence bag that was different from the others," Mackenzie said. "It was a different shape and a slightly different color. I was wondering if you could cross reference the acorns with the area of the park the bodies were found in. I'd also like to know if there are any that stand out to you for being different than the others."

"Your first question is going to be almost impossible," D'Amour said. "The vast majority of these acorns look to be from white oaks and chestnut oaks. These, along with a few laurel oaks, are going to be what make up at least eighty percent of the acorn-producing trees in Little Hill State Park. I can almost guarantee you that these acorns would have been on the ground at any of the sites."

"Okay," Mackenzie said. "You said the white, chestnut, and laurels are pretty common. Are there any oddities in the piles?"

D'Amour pointed to a pile where he had pushed three acorns away from the others. Mackenzie was pretty sure one of them was the same one she had spied in the evidence bag that had first aroused her suspicion.

"One of these, as you can see, is a little too worn to make a good estimate," D'Amour said. "But I think it's the same as the other two. These acorns come from a swamp chestnut oak. You can tell from the color, the almost fat bulge to the body of it, and the toughness along the crown. As far as I know, there aren't any of these anywhere in the park. Swamp chestnut trees tend to grow best in moist locations. Sometimes you'll see them along the banks of rivers in the South. Or, as the name suggests, in swampy or marshy regions."

"And are there any acorns like that in the park?" Bryers asked from behind Mackenzie.

"No, not that I know of," D'Amour said. "But there may be a few scattered along the outskirts of the park—back toward the western corner of the property. Out there, some of the trees get scraggly."

"Is there a river or swamp out there?" Mackenzie asked.

"There's a little creek that winds through it all but it never gets big or smooth enough to be considered a river," D'Amour answered. "Many years ago, before laws buckled down on the use of public parks, people used to camp out there and go frog gigging. When there was that homeless problem, some of the homeless stayed out there in little shacks that were put up just outside of the park's boundaries. Those shacks were built by hunters but never got much use other than from the homeless and adventurous frog giggers."

"What the hell is frog gigging?" Bryers asked.

"Ever eaten frog legs?" D'Amour asked.

"Can't say that I have. I've heard of people eating them, though."

"Frog gigging is going out near marshy areas or creek beds and hunting for frogs. It's mostly done with pitchforks. A lot of that kind of stuff used to go on in the Deep South not too long ago."

"Do you think there would be any swamp chestnut oaks out there?" Mackenzie asked.

"Oh, I can almost guarantee it. That would be the only place I could think of within the whole park where they'd grow. You'll know them by sight because they tend to grow a little smaller. The branches typically sprout a little lower to the ground that most other oaks. And there should be lots of acorns on the ground around them because the acorns of the swamp chestnut oak mature in just one season."

Mackenzie took the three acorns in question and pocketed them. "You said this area is on the western edge of the park?"

"Yup."

"How far?"

D'Amour shrugged but still looked very excited. Mackenzie assumed that a man with a botanist background that spent his time studying trees and seeds usually didn't get involved in this sort of thing very often. "About twenty miles from here," he answered. "About fifteen or so from the main entrance of the park."

"Can you show me where on a map?"

D'Amour went into his desk drawers and pulled out a map of the park which he spread out on his desk. He skimmed his fingers over the paper and tapped at a location on the left edge of the page. "Right there."

"And those shacks are still up?" Mackenzie asked.

"To the best of my knowledge."

Mackenzie and Bryers exchanged a look. He nodded.

This might just be where the killer was.

CHAPTER THIRTY FOUR

When Mackenzie stepped into the forest half an hour later, it felt much different than the first time she and Bryers had entered Little Hill State Park. By taking Barry D'Amour's route, she and Bryers were able to guide the agency sedan carefully down an old stripped logging road. The dirt track branched off of the main road three miles away from the western perimeter of Little Hill's border. As they headed down it, the growing morning light looked dusty and almost apocalyptic.

The road was rough but passable. Still, it took her ten minutes to cover the mile and a half or so that ended at a small dead field. The logging road kept going on beyond the field but this was the spot where D'Amour and Andrews had told them to stop. From here, they were to walk on foot into the forest until they came to the edge of the park's perimeter about a mile or so into the forest.

When she took her first step into the woods with Bryers by her side, she turned and looked back to the dead field. The sedan looked alien sitting there, like some spaceship from an advanced land.

"You okay?" Bryers asked her.

"Yeah. It's just very quiet."

"You think this acorn thing is the answer to it, don't you?" he asked as they walked deeper into the forest.

"I think there's a good chance," she said. "My hope is that in his habitual acorn-collecting, Albrecht just happened to pick one up when he met with whoever it is that he is helping."

"So you're convinced Albrecht wasn't the killer?"

"Almost one hundred percent. But if we get out here and somehow find otherwise, I'll be the first to apologize to Clements."

Bryers nodded his agreement. When he did, she saw that his eyes looked tired. It might have been her imagination, but she was pretty sure he was also laboring a little too hard to draw in his breath. But he forged on without complaining. He stayed directly behind Mackenzie, never further than two steps behind.

She scanned the area for trees that matched the picture she had pulled up on her phone on the way out here. So far, though, she saw nothing that resembled a swamp chestnut oak. D'Amour had told them that she'd probably have to walk at least a mile or more until she started seeing them.

They walked on in silence. As they did, Mackenzie couldn't help but wonder what Kirk Peterson was up to at that moment. Because of the time difference, he was probably still sleeping right now, but she wondered what else he had come across in the Jimmy Scotts case. That then led to her conversation with McGrath; she was still in a glad sort of shock over the fact that he was subtly giving her the go-ahead to take the Scotts case and, as a result, her father's reopened case. She wondered if he was doing it because he was starting to believe in her or if he was setting her up to fail.

She shook the thought off when she noticed a scattering of acorns on the ground. She knelt down and picked them up, sorting through them. None of them were a match to her swamp chestnut.

As they walked further on, Mackenzie started to wonder what sort of killer would need an assistant to kidnap his victims. While Will Albrecht had never actually come out and admitted to it, she was fairly certain it was the case. Even Clements and Smith had seemed to believe it, too. Of course, that had been during the excitement of the revelation that Charlie Holt had been Will Albrecht all along. In that moment of jubilation, they may have agreed with just about anything.

Thinking about how a man could so easily swerve his abductee made Mackenzie think that they were dealing with a man who had a charismatic sort of charm—especially to corrupt a child into thinking that the act of killing was part of a very important work. That it was not just okay, but necessary.

Got to be careful, she thought. *This guy is more than just a killer. He's damned smart, too.*

The brutal styles of the killings…having an accomplice…knowing the woods well. This was something he had planned out for a very long time. And that made him all the more unpredictable.

She was broken from her train of thought by Bryers's voice behind her. It was harsh and ragged.

"Got to stop," he said.

"Are you okay?" She turned around and saw that he was beyond winded and growing pale.

"I will be," he said, taking a seat on a nearby stump. "I just need to catch my breath. My lungs are burning. Chest feels a little tight. It's happened before, so I know it'll pass. You go on ahead, though. See what you can find. I told you I would make sure I didn't hinder your progress."

"Well, I can't just leave you here," Mackenzie argued.

"Sure you can. Just make a point to come back and find me. And for God's sake…if you *do* find something, don't be a hero. Come back for me and we'll take it together…or call for backup from Clements."

Mackenzie considered this for a moment before finally nodding and continuing on. She figured there was nothing that could happen to him while sitting alone on the stump. The car was less than half a mile behind them. And if she *did* come upon something questionable, she would just turn back and they could regroup.

"Yell for me if you need me," she said.

"Yes ma'am. But don't worry about me," he said, patting his sidearm. "I'll be fine."

Mackenzie continued on, walking through the forests as the morning sun filtered through the branches overhead. She found herself growing anxious with the passing of each moment. She then realized that she had reached into her pocket and started to roll one of the acorns between her fingers. An eerie chill passed through her and she quickly pocketed it again.

She looked into the woods ahead of her and tried to picture the scene…how Will Albrecht had come across the swamp chestnut acorns. Did he meet with the killer out here somewhere? Was there a lair of sorts somewhere ahead of her where Will met with the killer? Did the killer give Will instructions? Who to take? How to take them? She tried to picture Will out here somewhere, speaking with the killer and absently picking up an acorn that was slightly different in appearance than the others he had picked up and nervously picked and peeled at.

Out here in the quiet of the forest, it was actually quite easy to imagine.

She carried on and had walked perhaps another twenty minutes when she saw the first swamp chestnut tree. It looked exactly like the picture Barry D'Amour had showed her. It was mostly stripped of its foliage; she could see the dark lumps on the ground, the almost circular shapes of the acorns scattered along with the leaves.

She went to one and picked it up. She compared it to the acorns in her pockets and found that it was an exact match. She looked ahead and saw several other swamp chestnut trees. They weren't as numerous as the other types of oaks and firs standing all around, but they seemed to grow in number the further into the woods she peered.

She followed them like a trail, realizing that her pace had slowed. The swamp chestnuts seemed ominous to her, like a signal that something was wrong here…

After another three minutes, the ground dropped off slightly. Just ahead of her, she saw the muddy banks of the meandering creek D'Amour had mentioned. Further along it, she saw an old dilapidated shack. It looked almost like an outhouse. Its roof was mostly caved in and the boards were rotted. This, she assumed, was one of the old frog gigging shacks D'Amour had told them about.

She took a few steps toward it and before she reached it, she spotted another structure on the other side of the creek. It sat on a little plot of land directly in front of a rise in the land where bits of rock pocked through the ground. This structure was larger than the gigging shack she'd seen. It looked almost like a primitive cabin—some recluse's old lean-to. But it had what almost served as a crooked little porch. A five-gallon bucket sat in front of it.

And from what Mackenzie could see from this distance, it looked like there had been recent movement in the foliage around the front of the shack.

Swamp chestnut trees surrounded the shack on all sides. The ground was covered in acorns all around it.

This is it, she thought.

Her hand went instinctively to the butt of her gun. She then thought of Bryers, sitting about a mile further back. She knew she should go back to him before venturing ahead.

But that ugly lean-to was right there, no more than thirty yards away from her.

She couldn't go back. Not now.

Walking as quietly as she could on the fallen leaves and twigs underfoot, Mackenzie started forward. Her eyes stayed on the shack even when she had to take a wide step over the creek.

When her feet were both securely on the other side, she felt like she had arrived…somewhere. Something was different on this side. Something was amiss. Her instinct kicked into overdrive and adrenaline started pumping into her blood in drastic amounts.

Still, she started forward again.

The forest was beyond quiet all around her—a silence she felt in her heart.

Yet she was still unable to hear the soft treading footsteps of someone approaching from a few feet behind her.

CHAPTER THIRTY FIVE

As Mackenzie closed in on the shack, she could smell something in the air. In fact, it was a few different smells. One she could instantly notice was the smell of human sweat and occupancy. The other was almost a chemical smell that she could not place right away. It wasn't very strong but seemed to intensify with every step she took toward the lean-to.

She stopped in front of it, feeling the urge to call out to see if anyone was there. She recalled the stories she'd heard about the homeless often coming out here and wondered if this was a shelter that had been left behind. She looked down to the ground in front of the shack and saw that her first guess had been correct—someone had been here recently.

She took another step and that's when she heard something behind her.

She turned quickly, her hand going for her gun.

When she saw the man coming at her quickly with an axe in his hand, she brought her gun out. Before she could steady it, she saw the axe coming down and had to sidestep it. She felt the rush of wind just inches from the side of her face as the swing went wide. Rather than shoot the man, she rushed at him as he recovered from his swing. She struck him squarely in the side in a tackle that would have made any defensive lineman proud.

They both went to the ground but when they did, the man rolled over hard and trapped her right hand beneath him. She lost her grip on the gun just as the man tried delivering an elbow into her face. She blocked it and wrenched his arm back. He shouted out in pain but fought back with an intensity that seemed much greater than his small stature.

It was the first time she managed to get a good look at him. He looked to be in his late fifties. He was tall and haggard, with a growth of gray hair on his chin that could not quite be called a beard. He had intense blue eyes that looked impossibly bright in contrast to his dirty tanned skin. There was something almost feral in his eyes that made Mackenzie wonder if she might not make it out of this alive.

He tried getting to his knees, using the head of the axe to push himself up. He gave a hard heave with it and Mackenzie felt herself being lifted from the ground. The man spun around but Mackenzie kept her grip on his arm, pulling it harder behind his back. The man roared, stumbled backward, and they both collided with a tree. The back of Mackenzie's skull connected squarely with it and her ears rang for a second.

The man tore free from her and wasted no time in hitching the axe back for another swing. His arm was hurt, though. The swing came slowly, allowing Mackenzie to duck. Before he even started the swing, she threw two hard jabs to the man's ribs. He doubled over and when he did, she pivoted, clenched her fist, and came up with a huge uppercut. It connected solidly under the man's jaw. He went staggering back, stumbling against the side of the lean-to. He blinked a few times, trying to clear his head as Mackenzie looked to the ground for her gun.

She saw it, but it was too far away—closer to the man with the axe than to her. She rushed forward, trying to take advantage of his dazed state. By the time he was aware that she was coming again, he wasn't able to defend himself. She threw a hard knee into his stomach and when he doubled over again, she wrapped an arm around his neck, hugging his head tight to her side. She then dropped to her knees, flipped him over onto his stomach and drove a hard elbow into the space between his shoulders.

"How dare you interrupt my work," he growled.

Mackenzie ignored him, trying to reach for her gun, which was now about three feet away. She leaned over and her right hand was able to retrieve it. As she brought it to her, though, the man managed to roll halfway over beneath her. His strength was crazy. Mackenzie drew back her fist to throw another blow to his face but she was not fast enough.

The head of the axe came up flat-side first. It struck her in the forehead with a quiet little *thud*. The man had not been able to put much force behind it so it did no real damage—but it sent her sprawling backward onto the ground.

As she tried to get up, again hearing a ringing in her ears, she saw that the man had dropped the axe and had grabbed her gun. He was slowly getting to his feet as he held it directly at her.

"Get up," the man said. "And do it slowly."

Shit, Mackenzie thought. *I should have gone back for Bryers. This is bad...*

She knew better than to try to bargain with a man that she had just beaten rather badly. So she got up slowly, checking her surroundings for a way out of this. So far, though, she could find nothing.

The man was smiling. He was favoring his left side, where Mackenzie had done the most damage, but hobbled forward with a lunatic's smile on his face. The hand that held the gun was shaking, making Mackenzie feel even more in danger.

"Now get inside," he said, gesturing toward the shack's crooked front door with the gun.

"Look," Mackenzie said. "I'm an FBI agent. If you do anything stupid, you're going to be in a world of trouble."

"That don't matter," the man said. "After I'm dead, the earth itself will reward me for what I've done. Now get your ass inside."

Mackenzie did as she was asked. She stepped into the shack and realized that the sharp chemical smell was coming from in here. She saw more buckets along the back of the small shack's wall. A few Mason jars sat there as well.

Moonshine, she thought. *That's the other thing I was smelling.*

"To the back and to the right," the man said from behind her. He nudged the gun into the small of her back to get her to move faster.

Mackenzie followed his directions. It took less than four steps to reach the back of the shack. There, at the back, she saw what looked like the fragment to an old barn door blocking off another room to the right. She went to it and pulled it open as he marched along behind her. When she pulled it open, she did so slowly. She was hoping to distract him, to perhaps wheel around with a palm strike to his head when the door was partially open. But the gun remained at her back and she didn't dare attempt such a thing.

When the door was opened, her heart sank. She saw another axe, a sledgehammer, and what looked like an old handheld wheat thresher propped against the wall. The floor was mostly dirt with plywood and old boards scattered here and there. An old bench sat to the back of the small room. A few empty Mason jars sat there, along with two large rocks and what looked like a lower jaw bone.

Dried blood was splattered everywhere. The room was lit only by the sunlight that came in through the shack's front door.

It was then that she saw that the sheet of plywood she had seen on the floor was tied down. One end of a series of ropes was tied to the plywood and the other to one of two short poles on either side of the room. The plywood was about six feet long and seemed to be hiding something—maybe some sort of informal cellar.

As she looked at this, she felt the gun come away from her back. Just as she felt the moment of relief, she felt the gun again. This time, though, she felt it in the back of her head. It was hard and had come fast.

Just as her knees gave out and white flares of light passed across her eyes, she realized that the man had slugged her in the back of the head with her Glock.

She blinked away the white flares as she hit the ground. She made the decision then and there to pretend to be knocked out. She almost didn't have to pretend but managed to hang on to consciousness, if only by a fragile thread.

The man dropped down beside her and checked to see if she was breathing. She felt his hands on her chest and his finger under her nose. He nudged her with his foot but she purposefully did not respond. She hoped he might set the gun aside within her reach. She did her best to keep her focus on that task at the center of her mind to keep the lure of unconsciousness away.

But instead, he carried the gun with him over to the bench against the wall. She watched him as he set the gun down on the bench and then started working on the ropes that kept the plywood down. As he started untying the ropes, someone started screaming from somewhere within the shack.

It took Mackenzie a while to understand that the screams were coming from under the plywood. As the man removed the plywood sheets, the screams grew louder.

The man reached into the hole in the ground, delivering three quick punches that silenced the screams. The screams were now nothing more than moans, words muffled by weeping and hitching breaths.

"This woman has screwed things up," the man said, speaking directly into the hole. "After you, she'll go as well."

A male moan came from the hole in the ground as the man reached into it. He started to haul someone out of the hole by the armpits. Although her vision was still hazy from the blow to the back of the head, Mackenzie was pretty sure it was Brian Woerner—only a bloodier and terrified version of the young man she had seen in pictures provided by his sister and mother.

Having fought with the killer already, she knew that he was strong and that it would take him no time at all to get Brian Woerner out of the hole in the ground. If she was going to get out of this, she was going to have to do it now.

She sprang up as quickly as she could and leaped at the killer. The moment she was on her feet, she realized she was dizzy and disoriented. As she propelled herself at him, the room seemed to spin. Still, her aim was mostly dead on; she threw her shoulder hard into the killer's chest. Brian Woerner was trapped between them as Mackenzie went to the dirt floor. Behind her, the contents of the bench shook and trembled. Something fell to the floor and she heard glass breaking.

She did her best to roll away from the tangled limbs of the killer and Brian Woerner. When she did, she felt a sharp and stinging pain in her knee. She had no idea what caused it, nor did she have time to investigate. She got to her feet, still dizzy from the blow to the head. She brought her right leg back, nearly falling over, and delivered it into the killer's chest. She drew the same leg back again, this time aiming for his head, but fell over this time. The blow barely connected and all it did was cause her to fall.

When she did, the entire lower half of her body fell into the hole in the ground. She was dimly aware of seeing her right knee, bloodied and shining. Apparently, one of the Mason jars had broken and she had rolled her knee directly into the broken glass.

The killer came at her again, stumbling over Brian to get to her. Brian apparently caught on to what was happening and tried to stop him; he caught a vicious right-handed blow to the side of his head as a result.

Mackenzie struggled her way out of the hole, her right knee a blaze of agony and the room still spinning. She felt like she might pass out any moment and felt herself growing nauseous.

A concussion. If that's the worst I get out of this, I'll consider myself lucky.

She stumbled forward toward the bench, reaching for her Glock. The killer met her just before her fingers wrapped around it. He tried throwing a knee into her ribs but she blocked it. He was then on top of her, pushing her to the ground. She fought as hard as she could but everything was spinning—the room, the killer's face, *everything.*

She reached for the bench but her gun was nowhere to be found. What she *did* find with her roaming hand was one of the Mason jars that had fallen but not broken. She grabbed it and brought it up fast and hard. When it connected with the killer's head, the glass exploded. Blood spilled right away, coming from a deep cut in his brow.

He was just dazed enough for her to push him off of her. He thudded to the floor and instantly started scrambling for the gun. Mackenzie dove at him but he had already grabbed the gun. The two of them wrestled for possession of the weapon. She threw an elbow into his throat and he delivered a knee to her stomach. They struggled, gasping and writhing, until the killer threw a kick into her injured knee.

The glass that had cut into her was driven further into her knee. She screamed and lost possession of the gun.

Her scream filled the little room and seemed to cause the shack to tremble.

The only other noise that could be heard was a gunshot, which promptly put an end to her screaming.

CHAPTER THIRTY SIX

With a scream of pain coming out of her throat, Mackenzie heard the gunshot. Blood washed over her in a fast, brief splash. She closed her mouth and fell to the floor, certain that she'd been shot, sure that the pain would start registering at any moment.

Instead, the killer fell on top of her. Just as he came down, she caught a brief glimpse of his face—and, more than that, the neat little red hole in his forehead.

Grunting in frustration and anger, Mackenzie shoved the man off of her. She slid backward and looked toward the small doorway.

Bryers stood there, leaning against the doorframe with his Glock in his hands.

He was surveying the room with something like horror as Mackenzie slid over to Brian Woerner. He had fallen back to the ground, his left arm dangling into the hole in the floor.

He was still coherent, his eyes looking wildly around the small room.

"Brian Woerner?" she asked.

He nodded and then began to cry. He took in deep lungfuls of air and expelled them in what was almost hysterical weeping. Then, in a flash of movement so fast that it was uncanny, Brian launched himself on top of the killer. He started slapping him in the face and tearing at the man's skin. He screamed in a furious sort of howl as he attacked again and again.

Bryers came into the room and wrestled him away. Again, Brian started to weep but this time he remained crouched on the floor, unmoving.

Bryers ambled over to Mackenzie and put an arm around her. "You okay?" he asked.

"Concussion, I think," she said. "And my right knee is pretty messed up."

"What happened to coming back for me?" he asked.

Mackenzie said nothing. She found herself looking down into the hole in the ground. It was about three and a half feet deep. She wondered how many people had been down there. Hopefully it had only been the people they had discovered so far. She prayed there weren't more scattered body parts hidden around Little Hill State Park.

She tried getting to her feet and was relieved to find that she could. Her right knee would not straighten out but she was pretty sure there was nothing too serious going on with it. She might need stitches, but that was about it.

"You got your wind back pretty quickly, I see," Mackenzie said. "Good thing for me, I guess."

"I couldn't let you have all of the fun," he joked.

Together, they helped Brian gather his wits and led him out of the shack. He had been stripped down to his boxer shorts and his clothes were nowhere to be found. Bryers called the situation in to Clements and Smith after several attempts, fighting with the terrible cell phone reception so far out in the woods.

Mackenzie listened to him as she sat propped against a swamp chestnut tree. Through gritted teeth, she plucked shards of glass from her knee and tossed them to the ground. It hurt like hell and her head was still ringing. She knew that she was lucky to be alive.

Brian Woerner sat beside her, staring out into the woods. There was a blank look on his face and she knew he would be spending some time with a psychiatrist in the near future. She had tried speaking to him several times but whenever he would try to respond, he ended up crying.

Bryers came back over to them when his call was done. He looked very weak as he sat down next to her. He let out a whooping cough and frowned at her, as if apologizing that she had to hear it.

"So tell me what you think went down out here," Bryers said.

Mackenzie knew that he was trying to distract her from the pain in her knee and the dizziness that still wobbled her head. She appreciated it—she loved him for it a little.

"I'm assuming the killer brainwashed Will Albrecht after kidnapping him all those years ago," she said. "There might have been an almost paternal bond between them, seeing as how Will actually went to school, if those records you mentioned are indeed legit. I think the killer may have actually cared for him—or at least wanted to make it seem like he did. He must have eventually sold him on the idea that he was doing important work. We'll never really know what that work is…although he mentioned the earth rewarding him. Maybe he thought he was empowering the earth through the deaths."

"Yeah," Brian Woerner said. His voice was so unexpected that it startled Mackenzie a bit. "I heard him talking to someone about it. Returning flesh back to the earth before the flesh was dead. He was serving the earth…or something."

"And he wasn't the one that captured you, was he?" Mackenzie asked.

"No. It was someone else."

166

"Could you ID him if we showed you a picture?"

Brian nodded and stared back out to the forest. Apparently, he was done talking for now.

The three of them sat in silence, waiting for Clements and Smith to arrive. As they waited, Mackenzie reached out to the ground and plucked up an acorn. She rolled it between her fingers, cupped it in her palm, and then threw it with disgust out into the forest.

CHAPTER THIRTY SEVEN

Mackenzie's right knee was aching and itching as she sat in front of McGrath's desk. There were eight stitches in it and it was wrapped in layers of gauze. She watched as McGrath flipped through several sheets of paper with a machine-like approach. He'd been reading the contents of her report as well as documentation sent in by Clements and Smith for the last five minutes, asking only the briefest of questions as he read.

Finally, he slid the papers to the side and looked at Mackenzie with an expression she couldn't quite read. As usual, she wasn't sure what to expect from him.

"I don't know what to do with you, White," he said. "By all accounts, this case was a success. Despite your cowboy antics there at the end, you did what I asked. You wrapped up the case before another person was killed. More than that, you *saved* the would-be next victim and helped stop a killer. Beyond that, the men you worked with in Strasburg speak very highly of you—although this Clements guy says you are a hard-ass."

"With all due respect, sir, that sounds like a great report."

"It is. But I know your history. You have a habit of going out on things alone. You had no business leaving Bryers behind."

"I regret that, sir. But in the end, looking back on how it all played out, I think it might have been the best thing."

A long silence followed.

"So what now?" Mackenzie asked.

"What now," McGrath said, "is I show you that I am a man of my word. If you want to have a ghost presence on the Jimmy Scotts case out in Nebraska, it's yours."

She thought about it for a moment and let out a heavy sigh. "Can I have a day or so think about it?"

"You can have a week," he said. "If I don't hear anything from you by then, your chance is gone permanently."

"Thank you, sir."

"You're dismissed," McGrath said.

She got up from her chair with the crutch that she was quickly coming to hate and made her way to the office door.

"Agent White?"

"Yes, sir?" she asked, turning back to him as she reached the door.

"Damn good work. Keep it up—just not on your own."

She smiled. It felt good to hear those words. Somehow, it made her feel a future before her.

She nodded and made her exit, the aches in her knee highlighting his last comment.

***

Exactly sixteen days after rescuing Brian Woerner from the little shack in the woods outside of Little Hill, Mackenzie hobbled out to the street on crutches and caught a cab to the hospital.

In the back of the cab, she started to cry but kept it to a minimum.

As it turned out, Bryers had been too generous with the amount of time he had left.

He was currently having complications and the doctors weren't sure how much longer he was going to last. It was suggested by his doctors that the strenuous conditions of the events outside of Little Hill State Park had made his situation worse.

She got her sorrow out of the way, tears shed, and any questions of unfairness handled internally, before she reached the hospital. She took the elevator to the second floor and knocked on Bryers's door with the end of her crutch.

He was in bed, propped up on pillows and with clear tubes coming out of his nose. Surprisingly, he was in good spirits. She had been keeping him informed about the aftermath of the case via e-mail. It had been a good exercise for both of them during those three weeks. It was because of this that they had been able to fall into an easy discussion the moment she sat down.

"How much longer do you have to hobble around on that thing?" he asked her.

"Until it doesn't hurt to bend the knee," she answered. "The doctors were originally worried about nerve damage but it seems like I dodged that bullet."

"Good. Has McGrath come around yet?"

"Yes," she said. "I got a by-God compliment out of him."

"That's more proof for my side," Bryers said, reaching out and taking her hand. "You were made for this."

She wiped away a tear.

"What do you say you beat this thing and get back to work, old man?"

He shook his head sadly.

"Nah," Bryers said. "Even if I do get out of here, I'm done. I told McGrath everything this time. I sort of had to. If I don't show

169

up to work one day because I died...well, he'd eventually figure out what happened."

They both laughed about this and then fell into a silence. It was the same sort of silence that had held them while sitting in the forest outside of Little Hill State Park. It had gotten them through that difficult time and it did so now.

Ten minutes later, she gave his hand a squeeze. He didn't respond right away so she looked over to him. He was sleeping, his breaths coming in and out slowly, no doubt helped along by the equipment he was hooked into.

There was the faintest smile on his face as he slept. Mackenzie got up with the aid of her crutch, leaned over, and kissed him on the forehead.

She looked to that thin slumbering smile one more time before she left him.

It was the last time she saw Bryers alive.

Coming Soon!

Book #4 in the Mackenzie White mystery series

Blake Pierce

Blake Pierce is author of the bestselling RILEY PAGE mystery series, which includes six books (and counting). Blake Pierce is also the author of the MACKENZIE WHITE mystery series, comprising three books (and counting); of the AVERY BLACK mystery series, comprising three books (and counting); and of the new KERI LOCKE mystery series.

An avid reader and lifelong fan of the mystery and thriller genres, Blake loves to hear from you, so please feel free to visit www.blakepierceauthor.com to learn more and stay in touch.

BOOKS BY BLAKE PIERCE

RILEY PAIGE MYSTERY SERIES
ONCE GONE (Book #1)
ONCE TAKEN (Book #2)
ONCE CRAVED (Book #3)
ONCE LURED (Book #4)
ONCE HUNTED (Book #5)
ONCE PINED (Book #6)

MACKENZIE WHITE MYSTERY SERIES
BEFORE HE KILLS (Book #1)
BEFORE HE SEES (Book #2)
BEFORE HE COVETS (Book #3)

AVERY BLACK MYSTERY SERIES
CAUSE TO KILL (Book #1)
CAUSE TO RUN (Book #2)
CAUSE TO HIDE (Book #3)

KERI LOCKE MYSTERY SERIES
A TRACE OF DEATH (Book #1)

Printed in Great Britain
by Amazon

82563351R00102